CIAO

CIAO
ON THE RUNWAY

BESTSELLING AUTHOR
Melody Carlson

BOOK SIX

ZONDERVAN®

ZONDERVAN.com/
AUTHORTRACKER
follow your favorite authors

We want to hear from you. Please send your comments about this book to us in care of zreview@zondervan.com. Thank you.

ZONDERVAN

Ciao!
Copyright © 2011 by Melody Carlson

This title is also available as a Zondervan ebook.
Visit www.zondervan.com/ebooks.

Requests for information should be addressed to:

Zondervan, *Grand Rapids, Michigan 49530*

Library of Congress Cataloging-in-Publication Data

Carlson, Melody.
     Ciao! / Melody Carlson.
       p. cm. — (On the runway ; bk. 6)
     Summary: As the Forrester sisters take their fashion-focused reality television show to Milan, Erin gets the strong sense that her relationship with Blake is really over and Paige discovers that her fiance Dylan has cheated on her.
     ISBN 978-0-310-71791-1 (softcover)
     [1. Reality television programs—Fiction. 2. Television—Production and direction—Fiction. 3. Fashion—Fiction. 4. Sisters—Fiction. 5. Interpersonal relations—Fiction. 6. Christian life—Fiction.] I. Title.
PZ7.C216637Ci 2011
[Fic]—dc22   2011003258

Cover design: Jeff Gifford
Cover photo: Dan Davis Photography
Interior design and composition: Patrice Sheridan, Tina Henderson, Greg Johnson/Textbook Perfect

Printed in the United States of America

11 12 13 14 15 /DCI/ 21 20 19 18 17 16 15 14 13 12 11 10 9 8 7 6 5 4 3 2 1

CIAO

Chapter
1

Los Angeles is always hot in the summertime, but when July stays in the triple digits for a week straight, I am ready to evacuate to my grandma's house in the mountains.

"You can't leave me," Mollie protests as I'm visiting her and two-week-old baby Fern. "I'm stuck here and I would be totally lost without you."

"You guys could come with me," I say quietly as I rock the baby in my arms. Fern's almost asleep now, sucking on her pacifier, eyelashes fluttering on her cheeks.

Mollie chuckles. "Yeah, right. You've told me how your grandmother lives—it's like going back in time. No, thank you. Besides, what about your grandma's new boyfriend? She might not want any company with him around."

"That's possible." I lean over the side of Fern's crib, trying not to disturb her as I gently lay her down, adjusting her pacifier and tucking the baby blanket around her. Fortunately, Mollie's basement apartment stays nice and cool despite this heat wave.

Satisfied that Fern is down for the count, we go to the other side of the room where we open some sodas and I pop my *Britain's Got Style* disc into her DVD player. The episode already aired in England, but it won't be on our show until early August. "Like I told you, Paige was supposed to be a judge," I explain as Mollie turns on the TV.

"But she was nursing a hangover," Mollie fills in.

"Right. Anyway, I was wearing an earpiece, and Dylan was supposed to be feeding me fashion critique."

"Seriously?" She frowns at me.

"Yeah, it sounds lame now, but at the time it made sense."

"So what's going on with that jerk anyway?" She pauses the DVD. "Give me the dirt on Dylan."

I groan and lean back in the chair, trying to remember the latest development in the ongoing drama of Paige Forrester and Dylan Marceau's engagement. "Well, I already told you that he's been sending her flowers and chocolates and shoes—"

"*Shoes?*" Mollie's expression is a combination of outrage and lust.

"Oh, you know, nothing says 'I'm sorry' like a pair of Louboutins."

"Yeah, that red sole is like a big ol' bleeding heart." She takes a sip of soda and rolls her eyes. "So what's Paige's response?"

I shrug. "She finally had an actual conversation with him a couple days ago."

"*And?*" Mollie leans forward with way too much interest. But I have to forgive her. It's not easy being cooped up with a newborn 24/7.

"I think she's kind of torn. I mean, on the one hand, it's hard *not* to believe Dylan. I honestly thought he was in love with Paige too. And it's possible that Eliza set him up while we were in the Bahamas. We know she's capable of something like that."

"Maybe so, but wasn't it *his* choice to share a room with her?"

I nod. "Paige specifically asked him why he didn't just camp out in the lobby until the hurricane moved on."

Mollie nods. "And he said?"

"He said he didn't think it was that big a deal and that he didn't mean to fall asleep on the sofa, but it was late. And he said that Paige should just trust him."

Mollie laughs. "Trust him? Overnight in a hotel room with a beautiful woman? And let's not forget, she's a beautiful, *rich* woman."

"That's true." I recall Eliza's interest in remaining in the fashion world even though her modeling career fizzled. To be honest, this is one facet of the dilemma I hadn't fully considered before. But if Dylan's design firm really is struggling, as Paige has suggested, it's possible that linking himself to an heiress would be a tempting bailout plan.

"And you said that Eliza has had her eye on Dylan for a while, right?"

"Eliza was totally into Dylan during New York Fashion Week, and even more so when we stayed at her parents' chateau in France. And you should've seen Eliza in the Bahamas when she congratulated Paige on her engagement. She was pea green with envy."

"So ... what if it really was a setup?" Mollie asks in an intrigued tone. "What if Eliza planned the whole thing right from the start—a way to trap Dylan and hurt Paige?"

"I don't know. It seems a little far-fetched."

"But what if Eliza, knowing the hurricane was coming, talked Dylan into taking her to that other hotel where she already had the suite booked? Maybe she pretended she needed his help, somehow enticed him up to her room ... and then slipped him a Mickey." Mollie looks at me with wide eyes. "What do you think?"

I laugh. "I *think* you've been watching too many old Hitchcock movies."

"It could've happened. Then after it was all said and done, Eliza acted like they'd had a little tryst and—"

"But why wouldn't Dylan just say that?" I shake my head. "No, I think Paige is right. Maybe Dylan's been using her all along."

"You think he's used her to promote his clothing line?" Mollie purses her lips like she's ruminating over this. "Yeah, I guess that's believable. Paige Forrester *is* a hot commodity in the fashion world. A designer could do worse than engage himself to someone like her—even if it's just for a short spell."

"I really hate to think of Dylan like that."

"But he's a businessman, Erin. He has employees, and the bottom line. He might've rationalized that he was simply saving his ship."

"But how does he look now? I mean, if word gets out that he was just using Paige?" I ask her.

She frowns. "Good point. But maybe that's why he has to move on to another girl—one with a lot of money."

"I don't know, Mollie. That just makes it all so sad and pathetic, especially for Paige. It's like she was blindsided."

"Life's like that sometimes."

"I just didn't think Dylan was that kind of a guy."

Mollie sets down her soda with a clunk. "Guys are so flaky."

I'm tempted to point out that not all guys are like that. But I realize that will only start an argument and will also initiate Mollie's questions about my personal life. So far I haven't told her much about what's going on between Blake and me. In fact, I haven't told anyone—perhaps because I'm still trying to wrap my head around it myself. Am I really ready to be as serious as Blake seems to want? Do I want to take it to the next level?

"Speaking of flakes ..." I smirk at her. "How's old Tony boy?"

Mollie rolls her eyes.

"Blake tells me that Tony's been coming to visit you."

She tips her head toward the crib. "More like to visit his daughter."

"But that's kind of cool, isn't it?"

She makes a lopsided smile. "I guess."

"And when he comes to visit Fern, I suppose the two of you don't talk at all?"

She shrugs. "We talk, a little."

"So ... what have you been talking about?"

"I don't know." She shrugs and doesn't meet my eyes.

"Fine. Just keep on being tight-lipped about the whole thing. All you'll do is make me even more curious." I point my finger at her. "In fact, now I'm suspicious. I'll bet you two are getting back together, aren't you?"

She scowls at me. "No way."

"No way on your end, or no way on Tony's?"

"No way—on my end."

I blink. "Seriously?" I find this hard to believe, especially considering how she's been pining away for her ex for months.

She nods. "I told Tony that even if he begged me—if he

got down on his hands and knees and crawled over broken glass—I would still not go back to him."

"And what was his reaction to that?"

Her mouth twists to one side. "Probably relief."

"So does that mean he was *asking* you to go back to him?"

"Not exactly. He was more what-iffing. Like *what if* we got back together? *What if* we became a little family? Would it work?"

"Would it?"

Mollie's expression softens a bit. "Sometimes I wonder if it would."

"And?"

She laughs. "And then I wake up and realize I was just dreaming."

I actually feel relieved at this. Not that I wouldn't want Mollie to get back with Tony—if it's the right thing. But I've seen her hurt so badly, wounded so deeply ... I wouldn't want her to jump back into it again. "Well, anyway, I think it's cool that Tony is interested in seeing his daughter."

Mollie brightens. "And he's promised to pay child support too."

"Good for him."

She nods. "Yeah. But that means he can't move out of his parents' place like he'd been planning. And he'll have to keep working once school starts in the fall—just part-time, but he'll be pretty tied down."

"Not as tied down as you."

"That's true. But at least I'll be going back to school too. More than ever, I want to finish my degree now. I have to."

I want to ask her about acting, but hate to make her feel bad. I know becoming an actress had been her dream, and

12

that aspiration got set on the back burner during her pregnancy. Maybe it's dead and buried now.

"So what's going on with the show these days?" Mollie asks.

"Mostly we've been putting together the Bahamas shows," I tell her. "I'm still getting to intern in the editing room."

"Cool."

"Yeah, it's a great way to learn."

"So when does your show go on hiatus?"

"All of August. After that we'll get ready for Italy. Late September is Milan Fashion Week. It's supposed to be really good, and most of the top designers in the world will—"

Mollie holds up her hand. "Sorry I asked. That's all I need, you know, when I'm scrambling around here, changing stinky diapers and trying to keep up with my homework. It'll just totally make my day to imagine you and Paige roaming around Italy."

"Hey, if it turns out anything like the Bahamas trip, I'd rather be in your shoes, going to classes and taking care of Fern."

"Yeah, right. I'm sure there'll be a hurricane in Italy, Erin." Her voice drips with sarcasm. "No, you and Paige will be hobnobbing and shoe shopping and I'll be stuck here doing the laundry. Do you have any idea how many loads of laundry I do a week?"

I shrug.

She makes a dramatic groan. "You and Paige ... man, you guys have the life."

I wish I hadn't mentioned Milan to her. Sometimes I forget that Mollie still has some serious jealousy issues. "So maybe we shouldn't watch this DVD either."

"No, no, I want to see that. I have a feeling it'll be pretty funny."

"You mean that *I'll* be pretty funny?"

She grins as she aims her remote at the TV. "Hey, you've never claimed to be a fashion expert, Erin. So shoot me for wanting to see you floundering on an international TV show. I'm only human."

But as we watch *Britain's Got Style*, I can tell that Mollie is a bit disappointed. Not only do I not totally flounder, I get more camera time than Eliza. Plus I get some laughs—not all at my expense either.

"Who knew?" Mollie says once the show is over.

"Who knew what?"

"That Erin Forrester is finally starting to get fashion."

I glance at my watch. "And now Erin Forrester needs to get going." As I gather my stuff, I explain that I promised to visit our director, Fran, this evening and leave the DVD with her.

"How's she doing?" Mollie asks with concern.

"She's scheduled next Monday for her bone marrow transplant. She just needs to remain stabilized until then."

"Oh, good. I'll keep praying for her."

"She'll appreciate that." I hug Mollie and tell her good-bye then head outside. Despite the fact it's close to eight o'clock, the temperature still feels like it's in the high nineties.

Fran's out of the hospital and back in her apartment now. Her mom even flew in from Boston to stay with her awhile. She's only been here a few days, but it's obvious they don't get along too well, which is why I've been trying to drop in sometimes, just to lighten the otherwise heavy atmosphere. After all I've been through with Fran during her cancer treatments, I can't just turn away. Maybe it's my calling to help others. Whether it's Mollie, Fran, or Paige, it seems that I've been doing a lot of hand-holding lately. But I'm okay with it—I think it's what Jesus would do.

Chapter 2

I'm barely in the door at Fran's apartment when I realize that Mrs. Bishop is on some kind of tirade. As she lets me in, her cheeks are flushed and she's all worked up about something. "Come in, come in," she says in an aggravated tone.

"Mother's been trying to convince me to go home with her," Fran tells me from the sofa. She's wearing a forced smile and her eyes look tired.

"Only because it makes perfect sense." Mrs. Bishop is pacing back and forth between the tiny dining area and the living room. "I could care for you in the convenience of my own home and—"

"It would be convenient for you, Mother. Not for me." Fran is pushing herself to her feet, and I can tell she's struggling. I rush over to help, giving her my arm to pull herself up.

"We have excellent doctors and medical facilities in Boston." Mrs. Bishop stops walking, staring at us as I'm guiding Fran toward her room.

"I think Fran might need to go to bed," I say.

"Yes. Fine." Mrs. Bishop waves her hand in the way a queen might dismiss a servant. Then she follows as I slowly walk Fran down the short hallway. "But I want you to listen to me, Fran. There is nothing you have here in Los Angeles, well except for this stinking heat, that we don't have in Boston."

"Boston can get hot—"

"It's not hot now. I just spoke to your father and he says it's in the midseventies and there's a nice breeze—"

"Yes, Mother, and I'm glad the weather is nice there. But the point is, my doctors are *here*. And I'm scheduled to—"

"We have the finest doctors in the world in Boston, Francis Marie, and you know it."

We've arrive in Fran's bedroom, and I'm hoping that Mrs. Bishop will back off, but she doesn't. Whether it's the LA heat or her Bostonian stubbornness, this woman is relentless to-night. Finally, with Fran sitting breathlessly on the edge of her bed, I turn to Mrs. Bishop. "I know you love your daughter, but right now Fran needs some rest. So maybe you could have this conversation with her another time—when she's stronger."

Mrs. Bishop's brows arch, but fortunately she takes the hint and leaves the room. "Sorry," I say to Fran as I help her lie down, "I didn't mean to sound so bossy, but—"

"Bossy?" Fran lets out a weary chuckle as she leans back. "Who are you kidding? My mom wrote the book on bossy."

"Well, I just thought you needed a break."

She closes her eyes and sighs. "I did. Thanks."

"Can I get you anything?"

"Just some water and my pills over there on the dresser."

"How about something to go along with the pill?" I ask as she puts one in her mouth. I know how irritated her stomach has been since starting chemo again. "A little toast and yogurt maybe?"

She shrugs then washes the pill down with a sip of water.

"I'll take that as a yes," I say as she sets the water glass on her bedside stand. Then I return to the living room, where Mrs. Bishop has resumed her pacing. She reminds me of a bird. Not a dainty sort of bird — more like a chicken, with her rounded body and thin legs. And the jerky way she moves about, almost as if she's pecking, is kind of hen-like too.

"I'm getting Fran a snack," I tell her.

"She already had dinner."

"Great." I nod. "But it's good for her stomach to have a little food with her medicine."

"I suppose."

As I wait for the bread to turn to toast, I attempt to talk some sense into Mrs. Bishop. "You know, Fran is comfortable here in her apartment ... and with her doctors and Cedars-Sinai, and I don't think it would be in her best interest to move her just now."

"How old are you?" Mrs. Bishop demands out of the blue.

I blink. "Nineteen."

She laughs. "You're nineteen, with a role in a kids' reality show? What makes you think you're an expert on how to make my daughter well?"

Just then the toast pops up, and I distract myself by applying a very thin layer of butter, the way Fran likes it. I cut it into fourths and set it on a small plate. Then with the yogurt in one hand and the toast in the other, I face this outspoken woman. "It's true, I'm young. And I'm not an expert," I say evenly. "But I really do care about your daughter."

"Humph." She gives me a skeptical look. "I'm guessing

you care more about your job and that Fran is your meal ticket than you do—"

"*Excuse* me." I lock eyes with her, ready to hurl some facts at her. But instead I walk away. I take Fran's snack into her room, closing the door a little too loudly behind me.

"Let me guess," Fran says in a weary voice. "Mother is setting her sights on you now."

I shrug. "It's okay."

"Sorry."

"Just eat what you can," I say as I arrange the food on the tray and set it on her bed. I sit down and give her the update on Paige and Dylan. Naturally, I pad the story, making it seem more pleasant and hopeful than it really is. I suspect Fran knows there's more to it, but I decide perhaps this is a game we both have agreed to play ... the Pollyanna game. At least until she's better. I just hope that she *will* get better. I'm praying (and asking everyone else to pray too) that the transplant will work and turn things around for her. Because I have a feeling if things don't turn around, Fran won't last too long. I wonder if Fran's mom thinks about that.

When I'm sure that Fran's asleep I tiptoe out and find, to my relief, that Mrs. Bishop is not around. I suspect by the sound of the television that she's retired to the guest room for the evening. I let myself out, locking the door behind me. Then as I'm walking to my car I hit speed dial, finally returning Blake's call from earlier this evening.

"Hey, Erin." Blake's tone is warm and friendly.

I tell him where I am and what I've been doing, and he invites me to meet him for coffee on my way home. "Maybe an iced coffee," I say as I get into my Jeep.

"Great. I have something I want to talk to you about."

I tell him I'll be there in fifteen minutes. As I'm driving, I get curious. What is it that he wants to talk to me about? It's not like we don't talk a lot these days. In fact, since I got home from the Bahamas, we've been in closer contact than ever. I realize it's partly the result of the letter I wrote him, apologizing and confessing that I have some fears and inhibitions when it comes to relationships. It's like when I opened up to him, it opened a new door in our friendship. And now he wants to specifically talk about something.

It seems only natural to suppose that he wants to talk about *us*. Before I broke it off with him, he'd wanted to elevate our relationship to the next level. I'm curious if that's what he wants now. In some ways, I think I'd be open to committing to an exclusive relationship with him now. In fact, that might actually simplify life a bit. Like I'd know he was there for me, and I'd be there for him. No more playing games and guessing. Really, I'm thinking as I pull into a parking spot near Starbucks, that might be pretty cool.

"Hey, there you are!" Blake hugs me, kissing me on the cheek.

"How was work?" I ask as we go inside and get in line. Blake's been working this summer for an uncle with a landscaping business.

"Hot and grueling," he admits.

"But look at that tan," I say as I touch his cheek. "Hopefully you're using sunscreen."

He nods. "Yeah, my mom's been all over me about that."

We order our iced mochas then go sit down. Blake is grinning like he's got a sweet secret and I'm dying of curiosity, but I don't want to be pushy. Instead, I tell him about Fran's pushy mother. "She actually thought I was being nice to Fran just to secure my job. She said Fran was my meal ticket. Can you believe that?"

He laughs. "That just shows you how wrong the poor woman is."

"I guess." I smile at him. I'm not sure if it's just me or his tan or the fact that his hair is longer than usual, but it seems like Blake gets more handsome each day. I'm about to mention this when our mochas are ready and Blake goes to get them.

As he's walking back, I decide that if he is about to ask me to be in an exclusive relationship with him, I will definitely, absolutely, say yes!

"Here you go, my lady." He sets my drink in front of me and sits down.

I take a sip. "Mmm ... delish. Thanks!"

"And I'll bet you're wondering why I asked you here tonight."

"Yeah." I give him a hopeful smile and wait.

"Well, Ben called me this afternoon."

I blink. "Ben? Benjamin Kross?"

He smiles. "Yeah. Who else?"

I shrug and try not to show my disappointment, which is twofold. One part is that I suspect this conversation is not going to be about our relationship after all, and another part is that I really wish Blake and Ben would go their separate ways. It was sweet that Blake befriended Ben at first—back when Paige and Ben were dating, and when Ben needed a friend after Mia Renwick—Ben's reality show co-star—died. But when I saw him in France, it seemed that Ben was intent on returning to his selfish, shallow ways, and I can't imagine how Blake has any positive influence on him.

"Anyway ..." Blake smiles broadly. "Ben's in on the ground floor of a new reality show."

"A new reality show . . . just what this world needs," I say in a cynical tone that I instantly regret.

His smile fades. "So, it's okay for you and Paige to have a reality show, but no one else?"

"Sorry. That was just my exhaustion showing." I force a smile.

"Okay." He nods. "So anyway, Ben and his producer have been pitching this new show and it sounds like this one network is really interested, and—guess what?"

"I have no idea."

"Ben's invited me to be part of it." Blake is beaming now. "Can you believe that?"

I'm trying to wrap my head around all this. Ben wants Blake to be part of his reality show? "Seriously?"

"Yeah. It would be so cool, Erin. For starters, I could quit working for my uncle—talk about slave labor. Do you know how miserable it is to do yard work in this heat? Plus, I'll be able to make enough money to go to film school. I mean, later on, after the TV show ends."

I nod. I know how unhappy Blake's been with his dad's pressure to get a "real" degree. And how disappointing his first year of college was. Going to film school was Blake's dream even before it became mine. It seems that both our dreams got put on hold last year.

"Wow." I try to make a genuine-looking smile. "That's cool, Blake. Tell me about the show." It takes all my self-control not to rain on this parade, or jump to negative conclusions, or to point out that party-boy Benjamin Kross's show will probably end up a train wreck.

"It's called *Celebrity Blind Date*."

"*Celebrity Blind Date*?"

"Yeah. There'll be an ongoing cast of guys and girls who are semi-known, you know, kinda celebrities — like B-listers." He chuckles. "Actually they're more like C- or D-listers. And with the aid of a computer dating service, which will be one of the show's sponsors, they'll go on blind dates."

"Real blind dates?"

"Well, as real as anything can be in reality TV. Naturally, the cameras will be around, but Ben wants them to be sort of incognito. And at the beginning and ending of each episode the daters — "

"The daters?"

"You know, the regular cast — the pseudocelebs. Anyway, they'll gather somewhere, like a restaurant or club, and they'll discuss the dates — like what went wrong or right or whatever."

"It actually sounds like an interesting premise."

"It is!" His face lights up.

"And so did you tell Ben you would do this — for sure?" I'm hoping there's still a chance for Blake to escape the crazy world of reality TV.

"I told him I wanted to think about it."

"And what *do* you think?" It's a silly question, because I can tell by his expression that he's already on board.

"It's a huge opportunity, Erin. I think I want a piece of the action." He gets a thoughtful look. "But I'm curious ... what do *you* think about it?"

"Really?"

"Sure, you're my best friend, Erin. I want your opinion."

"Well ..." I pause to consider my words. I don't want to ruin this for him. "You know how a reality show can mess with your life, Blake. You've seen the kinds of trials Paige and

23

I have gone through. And that being in the spotlight comes with a price."

"I know." He nods. "I've had a front row seat, Erin. I'm well aware of the downside of the business. I'd be going in with my eyes wide open."

"Well, at least as wide open as possible," I caution. "But you never know what's around the next corner, Blake. I mean, even this thing with Paige and Dylan—it's really a by-product of our show."

"Are you saying Paige wouldn't have gotten her heart broken if you guys weren't doing the show?" He studies me closely.

"Hmm . . . good point."

"Life is life, Erin. Whether it's on film or on the streets, it happens. And this blind date show—well, I'll admit it's not going to save the planet, but I still think it'll be good fun. And it will look great on my résumé for film school."

"That's what I keep hearing."

"So anyway. I think I'll call Ben and tell him to count me in."

"What will your dad say about this?"

Blake frowns. "Oh, you know, he'll give me his free lecture about the real world and how I need a real job—but I'm sure he'll back off once he sees my mind is set."

Seeing his mind *is* set, I decide not to point out any more potential pitfalls to his plan. "So when do you think it'll go into production?"

"Assuming the network gives him the thumbs-up, Ben said he wants to get it rolling as soon as possible. He's worried that someone else might try to snatch his idea."

"I'm curious, Blake. How do you see your faith playing into the whole thing?"

"My faith is part of who I am, Erin. And Ben actually appreciates that too. He said he wants me to be up front with it. It'll provide some interesting contrast within the show."

"Like you'll be the angelic boy amidst all the little devils?"

He chuckles. "Maybe not quite like that. But Ben wants to have a diverse cast."

"Meaning it won't just be a bunch of the old *Malibu Beach* kids—the ones who've outgrown that show?"

"He'll probably use a few of them. But he'll hire some new faces too."

Suddenly I feel very tired. "You know, it's been a long day," I tell him. "I should probably get going. And I need to check on Paige. She's still pretty fragile."

"When is she going public with the breakup?" Blake asks as he walks me to my Jeep.

"I'm not sure." I glance at him. "You didn't tell Ben, did you?"

"No. I promised you I wouldn't. You can trust me."

"Good." I sigh as I unlock my vehicle. "To be honest, I'm not totally sure they *are* breaking up."

"Are you kidding? After what Dylan pulled?"

I shake my finger under his nose. "Remember . . . innocent until proven guilty."

"Right." He leans down and kisses me on the cheek. "Be safe."

As I drive home, I'm mulling over two things. First and foremost is Blake's big news. And while I know this is a good career break for him and I should be happy, an unsettling cloak of worry wraps itself around me. What if this "opportunity" derails Blake? What if it unravels him the way I've seen it unravel so many others? The other thought nagging me right now is that brotherly peck Blake gave me as a good-night kiss. What did that mean anyway? That his interest toward me has suddenly cooled now that he's got a hot new project to leap into? And, if that's the case, how does that make me feel?

On my way up the stairs to the condo, I remember my hopeful expectation as I drove to Starbucks. I was actually getting ready to tell Blake, "Yes! I want to be in an exclusive relationship with you!" Now, instead of taking that next step, I'm trying to accept that my would-be boyfriend might be participating in a reality show about dating—*dating other girls!*

Chapter
3

As usual, I'm surprised at my sister's resilience. Either that or she's becoming very adept at concealing her real feelings about Dylan. But other than being a little quieter and more of a homebody, Paige seems to be bouncing back. However, like many things in life, appearances can be deceiving.

After previewing some of the Bahamas footage, as well as the Eco Show episode, which I snagged on my own, Helen invites Paige and me into her office. "I just love that little red-headed designer," Helen tells us with enthusiasm. "The one whose mom died of a drug overdose."

"Rhiannon Farley," I say. "Yes. Remember, we met her in New York over the winter?"

"Yes, I thought she seemed familiar." Helen adjusts her glasses as she writes something down. "Well, she's great on camera. She has a compelling story. And I would love for you girls to do a whole show about her." Helen pauses as if thinking. "Perhaps the show could feature a couple other new designers too—you know, fresh young faces, passion, enthusiasm, new blood." She smiles at us. "What do you think?"

"I love it," I tell her. I notice that Paige seems checked out just now and I wonder why. But I suspect that seeing the Bahamas on the big screen (including shots of the actual heartbreak hotel) is taking a toll on her. "I know we did a bit of this last winter, but we never devoted a whole show to new designers. I think our viewers would respond really well to it. It's like that old story—only in America."

"Exactly." Helen points her pen in the air. "Only in America. That's good, Erin. Maybe that's what we'll call that episode." She leans over to write it down then looks up. "By the way, have you seen Fran lately?"

I explain that I was with her last night and give a quick update about the upcoming transplant procedure.

"I'm hoping to get this new designer show in the can before hiatus," she says. "Maybe I should give your mother a call."

I nod. "Yes. It's her last week at work at Channel Five."

"Perfect. If all goes well, I think you girls can plan to pop on over to the Big Apple by late next week. Sound good?"

"Sounds great. Fran's transplant will be over by then too."

Helen frowns at Paige. "What about you? You sure are being quiet. Everything okay?"

Now I notice that Paige looks like she's seriously unraveling, and I can tell she's about to cry. "I—uh—I ..." she stammers. Helen doesn't know about what happened in the Bahamas with Dylan yet, and I realize this situation is way more complicated than I'd assumed. Suddenly Paige stands up. "I—uh—I need a moment."

"Okay ...?" Helen's brows arch as Paige makes a quick exit. Once the door is closed, Helen turns to me. "All right, Jiminy, tell me what's going on here and make it quick."

I press my lips together, wondering how much to say. Then I realize there's really no way to keep this a secret from Helen. So, without going into much detail, I hurry to spill the story.

"That rotten little brat." Helen makes a growling sound. "If I had any mafia connections, I'd send someone out to break that boy's legs."

"We don't know for certain that Dylan cheated," I say meekly. "After all, there was a hurricane — it was kind of crazy. And he claims he only slept on the couch in the girl's suite."

"Where there's smoke, there's fire." She lets out a foul word. "Poor Paige."

"Yeah, it's been hard on her." I realize I didn't mention the name of the girl involved. "And there's one more thing."

"What?"

"Rhiannon Farley's business partner is Eliza Wilton —"

"Yes, I caught that part in the film. Eliza used to model. And wasn't she friends with Taylor Mitchell?"

"Uh ... yeah." I had forgotten about Helen's familiarity with Eliza. "So, anyway, Eliza was the ... the *other* woman."

Helen frowns. "Oh, dear."

"Allegedly, I mean. The other woman, allegedly."

"Yes, well, that does put a damper on the 'Only in America' episode."

Now I feel torn. For Rhiannon's sake, I really want to do her story. But what about Paige?

"Well, maybe we need to rethink that idea." Helen points her pen at me. "Or ... maybe you should take your mother and the crew and get that show yourself, Erin." She smiles. "That's it. We'll send you on a solo mission. You did a great job with the Eco Show and —"

"Sorry about that," Paige reenters the room.

Helen waves her hand. "It's completely understandable. Erin just filled me in on the details." She makes a *tsk-tsk* sound. "And you have my complete sympathy. Furthermore, you're off the hook for the New York trip."

"Really?"

"Erin will cover that show on her own."

"What?" Paige looks at me with troubled eyes. "I'm not going?"

"I figured you wouldn't want to go, Paige. Considering that Rhiannon's partner is, well ... you know."

Paige stands up straighter. "What if I *want* to go, Helen?"

Helen smiles. "Then you'll go."

"Fine." Paige nods firmly. "Then I'll go."

"Great. You girls bring your mother in here on Monday—check with Sabrina for the time—and we'll go over the details."

With the meeting over, I stop by Sabrina's desk. Today she's dressed like she wants to audition for the next vampire movie, but I know that's just her style. I ask her for an appointment on Monday. "But not after one," I tell her. "Fran is having her bone marrow transplant that afternoon."

Sabrina makes a sympathetic smile. "Tell her hey for me, okay?"

"I will."

Monday's meeting is set for nine, and before long Paige and I are on our way home in her car. She's quiet as she navigates her way through rush hour traffic.

"Are you okay?" I ask. "I mean with the New York trip."

She scowls my way. "I can't believe Helen was going to send you alone, Erin—and that you were willing to go."

"Is that why you're being so quiet? You're upset about *that*? If it makes you feel any better, I wasn't too comfortable with the idea either. I just didn't want to lose the chance to do a show on Rhiannon. She's a great designer. I think she deserves a break like that. Don't you?"

"I guess."

"But you're mad at me anyway?"

"A little." She sighs. "Okay, that's just the tip of iceberg."

"I know. And it's understandable if you don't want to be around Eliza. In fact, maybe we could plan it so that your paths never cross."

"Or, maybe ..." Paige gets this slightly diabolical look, kind of like the time she sneaked a lab rat into Britney Rolland's locker in middle school. "We could plan it so they do."

"You *want* to see Eliza?"

"Maybe ..."

"What exactly do you have in mind?"

"Nothing exactly ... but maybe by next week I will."

"It won't be anything illegal, will it?"

She laughs. "No, of course not."

"Or dangerous or stupid?"

"I'm not a fool, Erin."

"Right ..." I remember Paige's irresponsible behavior when she got drunk in the Bahamas and couldn't film our show the following day because of her hangover. Not a fool? Wasn't that, like, just a couple of weeks ago?

As she drives us home, I think I can see the wheels spinning beneath her perfectly coiffed blonde head, and I'm feeling a little worried. Then I decide it might be best if I'm in the dark about the whole thing. Ignorance might very well be bliss.

"I can't believe I'm going to be sitting home alone on a Friday night," Paige says once we're home.

"But you didn't mind before," I say as we go inside.

"Before—when I thought I was still engaged."

"So does this mean you're really not getting back together?" I point to yesterday's bouquet of flowers. "If that's the case, maybe you should let Dylan in on it too."

"Oh, he knows how I feel." She drops her purse on the table with a clunk.

"How *do* you feel?" I ask. "I mean, sometimes it seems like you two are finished for good. And sometimes I'm not too sure."

"I told Dylan that if he can prove his love to me, if he can convince me that he was never with Eliza, then there's still a chance for us."

"How can he do that?"

She frowns with one hand on the fridge. "I'm not sure. In fact, he keeps asking me the same thing."

"And what do you tell him?"

"That he'll have to figure it out." She pulls out a pitcher of iced tea.

"Maybe it'll help to go to New York," I say as she pours a glass. "Maybe you guys can sit down and talk it out."

She looks skeptical as she takes a long sip. "Maybe."

To change the subject, which is beyond me anyway, I tell her about the reality show that Ben's invited Blake to participate in.

"How do you feel about that?" she asks.

I shrug. "Okay ... I guess."

"Seriously?" She frowns. "I thought you couldn't stand Ben."

"I don't hate him. I just hate some of the stunts he's pulled."

"And it doesn't bother you that Blake's still hanging with him?"

I press my lips together.

"It *does* bug you, doesn't it?" she challenges.

"Yeah. It does."

"I knew it."

"Not that there's much I can do about it."

"Did you tell Blake how you feel about the show?" She sets her glass on the counter and looks at me like she's suddenly turned into a relationship expert.

"I think I did."

"Then it seems like he'd want to rethink it."

"But it's a big opportunity for him." I pour myself a glass of tea as well. "And besides, the show might not even happen."

"Why not?"

"*Celebrity Blind Date?*" I frown. "It seems a little hokey, don't you think?"

"I actually think it sounds like a solid idea." Her brow creases. "In fact, I'm a little surprised Ben came up with it."

"Why?"

"Oh, you know, he always seemed more like a face—not exactly the brains behind things." She peers curiously at me and changes the subject. "You didn't tell Blake about Dylan and me, did you?"

"No, of course not. Why would you think that?"

"It's just that I'm a little surprised Ben's including Blake."

"Why wouldn't he? I mean, they *are* friends. And Blake's been there for Ben a lot this past year."

"Yes, and that's nice on Blake's part, but it doesn't exactly qualify him to be on a TV show."

I frown. "It's a *reality* show, Paige. What qualifies anyone for that?"

"It's just that sometimes I wonder if Ben might be using Blake."

"*Using* Blake? For what possible purpose?"

"To get to me."

Normally, I'd point out how narcissistic that kind of thinking is, but because Paige is still pretty beat up over this Dylan dilemma, I decide not to mention it. "So what if Ben is using Blake?" I say. "Does it matter?"

"I guess not. As long as Blake is aware of Ben's motives."

"How could you possibly know what Ben's motives are?"

She gives me her "duh" look. "Because I *know* Ben. I know how that boy's mind works. Everything with Ben *is all about Ben.*"

I just nod. Although I hate to admit it, and I'd like to think she's evolved a bit more than this, I think that in some ways Ben and Paige are not all that different.

Chapter
4

On Saturday morning I call Mollie and offer to babysit Fern so Mollie can have some time off. But after I get there, Mollie has decided she doesn't want to go out. "I don't really have anywhere to go," she says.

"You can use my Jeep," I urge her. "The top's down. Just go out and drive around if you want."

"No, that's okay."

I study her. She's wearing rumpled sweats and her hair is pulled back in a scruffy ponytail. "Are you all right?"

"I'm fine. I just don't feel like going out."

"Have you even had a shower today?"

She frowns. "What? Do I smell?"

"No. You just don't look like yourself. Really, are you okay?"

She starts to cry.

"Mollie?" I question her. "What is it?"

"I don't know." She reaches for a tissue, sniffling.

"Did Tony do something?"

"No. Tony's been great." Now she's sobbing.

"Mollie?"

"I'm sorry—I can't help it." She blows her nose. "I just feel so sad."

"Did something happen today?"

"It's not just today, Erin." She wipes her eyes. "It's every day."

"*Every* day?"

She nods, blowing her nose again. "It's not that I don't love Fern." She strokes her baby's head. "I do. It's just that I'm so sad. Maybe I'm grieving."

"Grieving?"

"You know ... for doing this all wrong."

"Doing what wrong? You're a great mom, Mollie. You're doing it really right."

"No ... I mean having a baby without being married. Fern—she doesn't even have a daddy."

"She has a daddy, Mollie. Tony's her—"

"No, I mean she's—oh, you know what I mean." Now she's crying really hard, and Fern is starting to fuss too. I wonder if Fern's just reflecting her mom's sadness. I want to break this cycle.

"Mollie," I say in a firm tone. "You go take a shower and get dressed, okay?"

"But I—"

"Just do it!"

She blinks. "All right."

While she's showering, I go to her laptop and quickly google postpartum depression—or what they call the baby blues. I remember reading a brochure about this while Mollie was in the hospital with Fern. At the time I thought nothing of it, but after reading online a bit, I wonder if this is what's troubling Mollie.

I carry Fern upstairs, hoping Mollie's mom is still here. She looked like she was getting ready to go out when I arrived. Fortunately, she's still in the kitchen and it sounds like she's trying to get off the phone. I wait for her to hang up then ask if she has a minute.

"Sure." She makes a cooing sound at Fern. "How's my little princess?"

"I'm worried about Mollie," I tell her.

"Mollie?" She looks oblivious.

"I wonder if she might have postpartum depression."

Mrs. Tyson frowns. "Do you think so?"

"I know she's been a little moody since Fern was born, and I figured it was normal. But Mollie just admitted that she cries every day."

"Every day?"

"Do you think she should talk to someone about it? I mean, a professional?"

"She really cries every day?"

"Please, don't tell her that I told you," I say quickly. "I don't think she even wanted me to know. She wants to be strong for Fern's sake. But she is really sad underneath."

"Okay, I'll talk to her about it. And we'll make an appointment with her doctor."

"I'll try to get her to go out today," I say.

"Good luck with that." She shakes her head. "That girl's been a real stick-in-the-mud lately. I wanted her to come shopping with me today and she refused."

"Do you think that's part of her depression?"

"Maybe so." She glances at her watch. "I'm late, Erin. I'm supposed to meet a friend for lunch."

"But you'll make an appointment for her?"

"Sure." She kisses Fern then rushes out the door. I hurry back down to the basement and reach the final stair as Mollie is emerging from the bathroom. "Feel better?" I ask hopefully.

She just shrugs.

"Put on something fun," I tell her. "Like a sundress or something."

"Yeah, right." She gives me a dark scowl.

"Why not?"

She points to her bathrobe as if that's a clue.

"Huh?"

"I can't *fit* into any of my old clothes, Erin."

"But you look great, Mollie."

She rolls her eyes.

"Fine," I tell her. "Just put on a clean set of warm-ups and do something with your hair, okay?"

While Mollie's doing this, I change Fern's diaper then dress her in an adorable pink-and-white striped romper with a matching hat. "Hey, maybe we should do a *Runway* show about children's clothes," I call out to Mollie. She grumbles a response and I realize my work is going to be cut out for me today. That's when I decide to think like my sister. Better yet, I decide to call her.

"I need your help," I say quietly, even though Mollie's in the bathroom.

"What's up?"

I quickly explain about Mollie's blues. "I know it won't fix everything, but I was thinking if she had a little makeover, she might—"

"Great idea," Paige says cheerfully. And just like that she's concocting a plan, telling me to bring Mollie to the condo and explaining what we'll do after that. "You know—this would make a good show."

"Well, please, don't invite the camera crew," I tell her. "I don't think Mollie could handle that today."

"Mollie can't handle what?" Mollie asks as she emerges from the bathroom looking only slightly better than when she went in.

"A surprise," I say as I hand Fern to her. "I'll get the car seat and stroller."

"Where are we going?" she asks while she tucks some things into the diaper bag.

"You'll see."

We're almost out of the house when she glances in the mirror by the front door. "Oh, Erin, I can't go out looking like this."

"Don't worry," I assure her. "No one's going to see you like that."

"Huh?"

"Come on," I urge, "we have a schedule to keep."

Mollie relaxes a little when she sees we're only going to the condo. As we go up the stairs, I explain my little makeover plan. "Paige is going to help."

Mollie chuckles. "Well, that's a relief. I know you've come a long way in fashion, Erin, but I'm not sure I'd trust you with a makeover just yet."

"Yeah, fine." I make a face at her. "I'll just be the babysitter."

"Right this way," Paige says as soon as we're in the condo, waving Mollie over to where she's set up what looks like a hair and makeup station in the dining room.

"This is so sweet of—" Mollie's voice cracks in a sob.

"Now don't start crying," Paige warns her. "Your eyes are already puffy enough. Erin, go get a cucumber, okay?"

Before long, with cucumber slices secured by a sleeping mask over Mollie's eyes, Paige goes to work. "I tried to get you in to a couple of salons," Paige says as she spreads green gunk over Mollie's face. "But Saturday is a busy day. So I figured, why not just do it myself?"

"Don't worry," I assure Mollie. "You know you're in good hands. Paige is probably better than most of the pros anyway."

I take Fern into the living room, leaving Paige to work her magic. I know I'm not always appreciative of my sister's skills in the world of fashion and beauty, but I am today. And I know it can't substitute for an appointment with a medical professional, but I don't think it can hurt either.

After a little more than an hour, Mollie struts into the living room like a model. Okay, a short model. "What d'ya think?"

"Wow," I say quietly as I continue attempting to rock Fern to sleep. "You look like a new woman." Her usual unruly red curls are now silky and smooth and it looks like the ends have been trimmed, as well as some feathery bangs cut around her face that really bring out her eyes. Her skin is glowing, and her makeup is impeccable.

"I feel like a new woman."

"And now it's time to go shopping," Paige announces as she gets her purse.

"Maybe Fern and I should stay here," I suggest.

"No way," Paige says. "You're coming with us."

"But she's being a little fussy."

"That's because it's feeding time," Mollie explains.

So while Mollie feeds Fern, Paige and I gather up the baby things and switch them to Paige's car, which is a bit of an ordeal that I'm still getting used to, but I make sure Fern's seat is secure and safe. And before long we head off to one of Paige's favorite shops, where, as usual, Paige gets the full attention of the sales people.

"I really do think this could be a show," Paige says as she helps Mollie pick out some things to try on. Paige keeps in mind that Mollie is short and not necessarily "petite," picking out some items that make her look taller and thinner. She keeps the look more classic than trendy and, although it's still summer and warm, she looks for lightweight layers appropriate for the fall.

"Maybe we could call it 'Beating the Baby Blues,'" I say as I navigate Fern's stroller through a tight aisle.

"Maybe we could have you in it too," Paige suggests to Mollie. "Would you be willing to wear a pillow or something and pretend you're still pregnant?"

Mollie chuckles. "Well, I'm not eager to be pregnant again, but if I'm only acting, why not?"

"I'll tell Helen about this idea next week," Paige says as she hands Mollie a pale-yellow sundress. "Although I doubt we can do much with it before our New York trip."

"New York?" Mollie frowns. "I thought your next trip was Milan."

I quickly explain about Rhiannon and New York to Mollie, and before she can start getting bummed about our "fun and glamorous lives," Paige escorts her to the dressing room, telling her which things to try on with what.

After awhile, Mollie emerges in an outfit that really works—a shell-pink sleeveless top, a flouncy skirt in a fun, tropical print, and a light, lacy cardigan. "Very pretty," I tell her. "That color is great on you."

But Mollie looks glum.

"What's wrong?" I ask. "You look great."

"It's these clothes," she says. "They're too expensive."

I was expecting this, and I already have a plan. "We told you this is going to be part of a show," I tell her. "So the show is covering the cost of this outfit."

"Really?" Her eyes grow wide.

"That's right," Paige says as she holds out a pair of great-looking sandals. "Try these on, Mollie."

I realize what I said isn't completely true, but it's partly true. Because my money comes from the show, in essence, the show really is covering the cost. And, who knows? If we do a show about this maybe the costs *will* be covered.

Anyway, I'm glad to do this for Mollie. By the time the items are rung up, Mollie is beaming. She really does seem like a new woman as the saleswoman clips the tags and bags up her old clothes.

"Let's get some lunch," Paige suggests as we're putting Mollie's bags into the trunk. "I'll call and see if I can get us in somewhere special."

Before long, with Baby Fern sleeping contentedly in her stroller, we are dining al fresco at a new bistro. And after a couple of girls come up for autographs and photos of Paige, we manage to have a nice, quiet lunch.

"You guys are the best," Mollie tells us as Paige is driving back to her house. "I don't even know how to thank you."

"Well, first of all," Paige says firmly, "promise that you won't go around looking like you did when you showed up at the condo this morning."

Mollie laughs. "Sorry about that."

"Seriously," Paige tells her. "You need to realize that how you look will affect how you feel. Not only that, but it hurts my image too."

"*Your* image?" I stare at my sister. "Huh?"

"Well, Mollie's my friend too. I can't have my friends looking like something the cat dragged in. It's bad for my reputation."

Okay, I can't help but laugh. Leave it to my sister to make Mollie's postpartum depression all about her.

"I'll try harder," Mollie says. "And I'm honored that you consider me a friend, Paige."

"Well, of course you're a friend," Paige assures her. "Any friend of Erin's is a friend of mine. Right, Erin?"

"Right."

As I help Mollie lug the baby things into her house, I realize that Paige really doesn't have many friends. Not real ones anyway. Most of Paige's friendships have been ruined by jealousy or competition ... or just plain neglect on Paige's part. In fact, besides Mom and me, I can't even think of one really good female friend she has. While I was assuming that today was a generous sacrifice on Paige's part, I'm now wondering if she might've actually enjoyed the whole thing more than I realized.

As Paige drives us back to the condo, Blake calls my cell phone.

"Good news," he says happily.

"What's that?"

"The show—it's a go!"

"Congratulations," I tell him.

"We'll go into production in early August."

"That's great."

"So I thought maybe you'd want to go out with me to celebrate tonight."

"Sure, sounds good."

"Because I was thinking you're part of the reason this is even happening."

"Really? How's that?"

"Well, it's because of your show that I met Ben."

"Oh, yeah. I hope that's really a good thing."

He laughs easily. "Sure, it's a good thing."

Then he asks what I'm doing and I tell him about how Paige and I gave Mollie a makeover. "She was totally bummed this morning," I say as Paige pulls into the condo lot. "But she was on top of the world when we dropped her at home." I'm thinking that shopping might be preferable to drugs when it comes to beating the baby blues—except it can be expensive.

"Hey, maybe she'd like to come to dinner too," he says, "and I could invite Tony."

"Really? Are you sure that's a good idea?"

"Sure. Maybe Paige would want to come too. The more the merrier."

"You're sure?"

"Yeah. I want to celebrate. You check with them and get back to me. Okay?"

"Okay."

After I hang up I tell Paige about Blake's good news as well as his invitation. "He wants to celebrate."

"Really?" She looks touched. "And he wants me to come too?"

"Of course. Remember what you said—any friend of mine is a friend of yours."

"I think that sounds fun. Count me in."

When I check with Mollie, she's ecstatic. "That would be fantastic!" she gushes. "This has been the best day ever, Erin. Really, I feel so hopeful, like there really is life after baby."

"Of course there is."

"Anyway, I'll see if Mom can watch Fern. Can I get back to you?"

Finally it's set and I tell Blake we girls will meet him at the restaurant at eight. Although I'm not that thrilled about the *Celebrity Blind Date* show in general, I am excited for Blake. I think it's a big break for him. And I plan to be a good friend and show him my support.

Of course, underneath all this—ironic, considering my heel-dragging history—I'm feeling a little bummed that, in light of this new dating show, Blake and I aren't making any plans to move into a more committed or exclusive relationship. I know I should be relieved about this status quo, but the truth is I'm not. Go figure.

Chapter
5

"*I guess I'm kind of like the chauffeur and* chaperone tonight," Paige says as Mollie gets into the backseat of her car.

"What makes you think you're the chaperone?" Mollie asks.

"Because you girls have dates."

"It's not like that," I protest. "Blake just invited us all as his friends. And Tony's his friend."

"That's right," Mollie agrees. "Tony and I are definitely not dating. Not yet. Maybe not ever."

"Okay. Just five friends having dinner." Paige nods as if this concept is much more appealing.

But we get to the restaurant, and the parking valet is just pulling away when we spot Benjamin Kross getting out of his car. "What is he doing here?" Paige hisses at me.

"I have no idea."

"Hello, ladies," Ben says. "Blake probably didn't get a chance to warn you I was crashing the party tonight. I hope no one minds." He's looking directly at Paige and she looks like she'd like to hit someone. Hopefully not me.

And then, just like that, she recovers. "Hello, Benjamin. I didn't expect to see you tonight."

"Do you mind?" he asks in a way that suggests he really does care.

She shrugs, adjusts her purse, and makes a stiff smile. "It's a free country."

"Before we go inside," he says quietly, glancing over his shoulder as if he expects someone to pounce on him, "I want to say something—to both you and Erin."

"Go for it." Paige stands tall, waiting. I'm curious too. Mollie, however, looks slightly starstruck. I remember she's always been a *Malibu Beach* fan and hasn't ever met Ben in person.

"First of all, I want to apologize to both of you for how I acted in France. I know I was a jerk, and I drank too much, and I'm really sorry."

I blink then stare at him. Is this really Benjamin Kross? Or is it his nice twin brother?

"I accept your apology," Paige says.

"Me too," I add.

"Thank you." He tips his head. "I think I need more good influences in my life."

Paige gives me a quick sideways look, like she's feeling lost too.

"And I want to congratulate you on your engagement," he says to Paige. "Dylan is one lucky guy."

"Thank you," she says stiffly.

"This is my good friend, Mollie Tyson," I say to him, for lack of anything else, and hoping to redirect the subject.

"Nice to meet you, Mollie," he says as he opens the door for us. "Shall we go inside?"

Paige and I exchange curious glances as we head into the restaurant. Before long Blake joins us, greeting us all with hugs and then leading us to our table. "Is Paige okay with Ben being here?" he whispers in my ear as he helps me with my chair. I simply nod and smile.

"This is awesome." Blake grins from the head of the table. "I'm so happy you all could come for my little celebration." He picks up his water glass, holding it up in a toast. "Here's to Ben for successfully pitching this idea. Kudos, man!"

Everyone lifts their glasses, then Ben points to Blake. "You guys probably know that Blake had a lot to do with this idea."

"Really?" I look from Ben to Blake. "I thought this was your idea, Ben."

"We kind of hatched it together," Ben tells me. "But I never would've come up with it without Blake's help. Did he tell you how we landed on it?"

"No." I shake my head. "I'd like to hear."

Ben points to me. "It was partly your fault, Erin."

I blink. "My fault?"

Ben nods. "Yes. When you dumped Blake—"

"Wait a minute," I interrupt. "I dumped Blake? That sounds a little harsh."

Blake has a sheepish grin. "Well, we sort of parted ways there for a while," he says. "It kinda felt like I was dumped when you went to the Bahamas."

"Oh, yeah," Ben looks at Paige. "How was the Bahamas?"

She smiles. "Well, other than a little hurricane ... okay."

"I saw photos of you and Dylan there. Looked like you guys were having a good time," Ben says to her. "Still being relentlessly pursued by the paparazzi?"

Suddenly I'm worried. What if Ben also saw photos of

Dylan and Eliza in the Bahamas? So far I haven't heard of any surfacing, but you never know. And if anyone would pick up on something skanky like that, it would probably be Ben. Or at least the "old" Ben. I'm not too sure about this new nice guy.

Fortunately, we get distracted as the waiter comes and starts taking our orders. As soon as he finishes, I turn back to Blake. "Now about your TV show," I say quickly, hoping to keep the topic away from the Bahamas and Dylan and Eliza. "I want to know what it has to do with me."

Blake laughs nervously. "Well, I was bummed about breaking up with you," he says with a sad expression. "So I told Ben I needed to do something to forget you."

"And I set Blake up on a blind date," Ben announces. "A blind date from—"

"You went on a blind date?" I demand. "Seriously? A blind date?"

"It was terrible," Blake assures me. "And besides, I thought we were done, Erin. I was hurting."

I nod. "Yeah, I understand. I'm just surprised, that's all." Okay, maybe I'm a little hurt too. But what did I expect? Blake's right; we weren't together. He had every right to go out with someone else.

"It was the worst night," Blake tells me. He goes on about how this girl, one of the lesser-known girls from *Malibu Beach*, was more into Ben than Blake, and how she assumed she was going out with Ben. "And she was mad right from the start, but she was trying to hide it. At first, anyway. But as the evening wore on she stopped making any effort to hide her disappointment. I kept trying to be nice, thinking I'd win her over or at least make it a little less of a disaster, but it wasn't working.

Then finally, just before dessert, she complained about one last thing and I got totally fed up."

"Blake walked out and left her with the check," Ben says, stifling his laughter. We're all laughing too.

Blake looks embarrassed. "I didn't really mean to do that, but she was so obnoxious and rude, I couldn't take any more."

"Plus, she could afford it," Ben assures us over our laughter.

"So I got to thinking how that would be pretty funny for a reality show," Blake explains. "I told Ben about it and we started brainstorming. The next thing I knew, Ben was telling his producer about it."

"And my producer pitched it to a couple of networks. We actually had a little bidding war last week." Ben gives Blake a high five. "Way to go, man!"

Our food comes and I'm surprised at what a good time the six of us are having. Even Mollie and Tony are getting into the swing of things. And Ben is being incredibly sweet and nice. Really, it's kind of like a happy *Twilight Zone*.

"I think everyone at this table should be on the show at least once," Blake tells us. "Just for laughs."

"But Paige is engaged," Ben says. "That wouldn't be right."

She nods and takes a sip of her water.

"Okay, Paige is off the hook, but Tony and Mollie, you guys could go out on a blind date with someone else — just for fun. Seriously, going on a blind date is kind of like a wake-up call."

"Shows you how desperate you are?" Ben asks.

"Or how much better someone else is for you." Blake looks at me.

"So you'd want me to be on your show?" I ask. "Go on a blind date with some guy I've never met?"

Blake looks unsure.

"Why not?" Ben asks me. "It might make you appreciate good old Blake even more."

I smile at Blake. "I appreciate him just fine now."

"Hey, maybe we could do some kind of combination with your show and ours," Ben says to Paige. "Like you could do a fashion commentary or suggest some style tips or something."

Paige's eyes light up. "That could be fun. Maybe we could do minimakeovers of some of your dates before they go out."

Suddenly we're discussing all the possibilities and I'm wondering if perhaps this was Ben's angle all along. Was he trying to make a connection to our show to help boost his? Although I suppose, really, with *Malibu Beach* and the other things he's worked on, he has enough connections without us. I'm probably just being cynical.

Finally our little celebration is drawing to an end. We all thank Blake, who insists on picking up the bill. I know it will cost a couple weeks' hard labor as "lawn boy," but he doesn't seem to mind. I sure hope this new show doesn't go bust on him before it even launches. But that, I remind myself, is not my problem.

We give the parking valet our tickets and go outside, where it's still hot and balmy, to wait for our cars. Suddenly we're surrounded by cameras and paparazzi. Everyone does their best to field questions, and Ben even mentions that we're celebrating a new reality show.

"Can you tell us the name of the show?" someone calls out.

"Not yet." Ben puts his forefinger to his lips. "But soon."

"And are all of you involved in it?" calls out another one.

"We're all friends," Paige tells him. "And friends help out friends."

"Is it true that your engagement with Dylan Marceau is going through a rough spell?" a guy yells from the back of the group.

Paige momentarily looks like the proverbial deer in the headlights.

"Of course not," I yell back. "In fact, we're heading to New York next week and Paige will be with him there."

"That's right," Paige chimes in.

"Is your wedding date set?"

"Not yet." Now Paige flashes a big smile and waves her diamond ring at them. "But you'll be the first to know." I'm thinking it's a good thing she put her ring back on tonight. A ring-less finger brings questions in this town.

Paige's car arrives and we quickly say our good-byes. Most of the paparazzi trail Paige as she gets into the car. She simply smiles and waves, acting like these guys are her best friends. Then they race back to where Benjamin and the guys are waiting for their cars.

"They remind me of parasites," I mutter as Paige pulls out.

"That's a bit harsh," she tells me.

"Yes, considering they're giving you free publicity," Mollie adds. Then she giggles. "In fact, I rather enjoyed it."

"You would," I laugh. "Not exactly like changing diapers or cleaning spit-up, is it?"

"Speaking of babies, it's feeding time." Mollie moans. "I'm leaking."

"Leaking?" Paige looks alarmed.

"She breastfeeds the baby," I explain.

"Oh, too much information." Paige makes a disgusted face.

"Hey, it's perfectly normal," I say.

"Yeah, you might be a mother someday," Mollie shoots back.

"I don't know." Paige shakes her head. "I don't think so."

"Why not?" I ask her.

"Motherhood just sounds so demanding ... and *messy*."

Mollie snickers. "Well ... that's true. It is."

"Maybe someday," Paige says thoughtfully. "When I'm, like, forty."

"Yeah, that's not a bad plan," Mollie agrees. "I'm the last person to encourage anyone to rush into it."

After we drop Mollie off, I ask Paige if she was really okay having Ben there tonight. "I swear I had no idea he was coming," I tell her.

"I was shocked too," she admits. "But it was okay. I really think maybe he's changing."

"It sure seemed like it. I've never seen him be so nice."

"And you noticed he didn't drink a drop."

"Yeah. He seemed totally sober. He's pretty cool when he's sober."

"He told me that he's been going to Alcoholics Anonymous meetings."

"Seriously? AA?"

"That's what he said."

"Wow. That's cool."

"I'm a little worried about the photos though."

"Photos?"

"I'm sure the paparazzi got some shots of me with Ben — or they'll PhotoShop them to make them look like I'm with Ben."

"Oh? You mean you're worried about Dylan?"

"I don't really care what Dylan thinks," she huffs. "In a

way he deserves to be concerned. I'm more worried about my own reputation, Erin. I don't want to look like I'm cheating on my fiancée."

"But you weren't."

"I know that. And you know that."

"I know, but the rest of the world—at least the gullible ones—will believe what they see in the tabloids." I shake my head. "It's so unfair."

"Tell me about it."

"Do you think it was odd that there were so many paparazzi there?" I ask tentatively.

"What do you mean?"

"I mean, it was pretty convenient for Ben to spotlight the upcoming reality show. Do you think he could've set it up?"

"Oh, no, I don't think so. It's pretty normal for the paparazzi to roam the city on a Saturday night. I'm guessing someone at the restaurant called and tipped them. It must've been a slow night ... or else it's just early. No, Erin, I don't think Ben planned that."

"What about his invitation to include us in his show?" I can't help being skeptical—it's who I am. "Do you think that was his reason for crashing the dinner tonight? Just to make a publicity connection with us?"

"You are the little cynic, aren't you?"

"Hey, you said yourself you thought Ben might've been using Blake to get to you. Remember? Well, tonight could have that appearance—to a cynic anyway."

She snickers. "Maybe so. But Ben was quick to excuse me from their show, thanks to my so-called engagement."

"So-called or called-off?"

She laughs in a sad way. "I guess I'll have to figure that out next week." She glances my way. "And thanks for fielding that question for me. I really want to keep the whole thing under wraps—until I'm ready anyway."

"Do you think Eliza might say something?"

"Dylan promised me she'll keep her mouth shut."

"How can Dylan deliver on that?"

"Good question. Let's just say he's very motivated."

I lean back and sigh. "I had fun tonight."

"Me too."

I'm thinking, all in all, that it's been a very good day. And maybe I'm okay with Blake's involvement in the reality show. Not that it matters what I think. But, really, what could it hurt?

Chapter
6

It's never been easy to visit Fran, but it's ten times harder with her mom there. Still, I know it's what I need to do after church on Sunday. So after I drop Mollie and Fern at their house, I head over to Fran's. On my way there, I pray for both Fran and her mom, and when I knock on the door, I feel optimistic. But when Fran's mom opens the door, my positive thinking nosedives.

"Good," Mrs. Bishop says in a sour tone as she lets me in. "Maybe you can talk some sense into her."

"What's going on?" I ask Fran when I spy her curled in a corner of the couch, with a throw pulled up over her.

"Nothing." She makes a weak smile.

"I'm going to wash up," I say as I head for the bathroom. I know how important it is to keep germs away from Fran right now. Her immunity is down and I've just been around a bunch of people. I scrub up, almost as if I'm going to perform surgery, then go back out and sit in the chair across from her.

"How was church?" she asks.

"Pretty good." I give her a nutshell version, which she seems to appreciate. I can hear her mom doing something in the kitchen so I lower my voice and ask her why her mom's in a snit today.

She rolls her eyes. "Does there need to be a reason?"

I chuckle. "Maybe not."

"She wants me to check into the hospital today."

"Why?"

She shrugs. "Maybe she's tired of taking care of me."

"That's not true!" Mrs. Bishop snaps as she comes into the living room. "I have a perfectly good reason for wanting her to go in today."

"What is it?" I ask.

"Because I want the best possible outcome for Fran." She frowns. "And I think it will improve her chance of success to go in twenty-four hours before her transplant."

I look at Fran. "Is that true?"

"My doctor said it was up to me."

"Up to you *and your caregiver*," her mother adds.

"And you'd feel better if Fran went to the hospital today," I say for clarification. "I can understand that." I point to Fran. "So what are your reasons for not going in until tomorrow?"

She holds up a finger. "One—I can rest better at home." Another finger. "Two—I'm not exposed to as many germs."

I nod. "That's a good one."

"And three—it's my life."

Her mom storms off now, slamming the guest room door behind her.

"That makes sense to me," I tell Fran.

She sighs. "Thanks. It's reassuring to know you don't think I'm crazy."

"Your mom doesn't think you're crazy," I say. "I think she's just worried about you."

She nods wearily. "I know. But she has a rough way of showing it."

I change the subject by telling her about our New York trip.

"You're kidding." Her brow creases. "You're doing a show about Rhiannon and Paige is okay with that? What about the Eliza factor?"

"I think Paige might have a plan."

"Oh, dear."

"I made her assure me that it wasn't illegal, immoral, or dangerous."

Fran laughs. "Well, if it's good, be sure someone gets it on film."

"Speaking of reality TV, there's going to be a new show." I tell her about *Celebrity Blind Date*.

"That sounds like a fun show." She sighs. "I miss work."

"Well, this transplant is going to be a success," I say with manufactured confidence. "And then you'll be back to work in no time."

"I hope you're right."

"I've got everyone on our church prayer chain praying for you, Fran."

"I appreciate that."

She looks tired, and I'm worried I'm wearing her out. "Maybe you should get some rest."

"Yeah, probably."

"Would you rest better in your room?"

She barely smiles then nods. So I help her up and walk her to her room, putting a glass of water by her bed. "I'll be at the hospital tomorrow," I promise. "While you're getting the transplant, I'll be praying."

"Appreciate it," she says weakly.

I squeeze her hand. "Rest well."

She closes her eyes and I watch for a minute, thinking how frail she looks, like she's literally balancing between this world and the next . . . and I wonder if she's really ready for it. So I push myself beyond my comfort zone and pray aloud for her. Instead of only focusing on her physical health, I pray for her spiritual health too. I ask God to solidify his relationship with her. "Help Fran hold onto your hand," I pray, "and to know and believe that you are able to hold onto her no matter what comes her way. Connect her to you, Lord, so tightly that nothing can shake her loose." Then I say amen, and the corners of her lips curl up ever so slightly, and I leave.

Mrs. Bishop is doing her pacing thing again. I decide to make an attempt to smooth things over with this often cantankerous woman. "I understand how worried you must be about Fran," I begin.

She nods, her chin quivering. "I am."

"I'm sure it's hard on you. I remember how helpless I felt when I was taking care of her, like so much was riding on it. You know?"

"Yes!" she says eagerly. "That's just how I feel. I'm afraid I'm doing something wrong—and that she—she won't make it—and it will be my fault."

"You have to know that's not true. I mean, it's not like you're God."

She's wringing her hands. "But I have to wonder—why does God allow her to suffer like this? Children are supposed

to outlive their parents. I never imagined I might end up bury-
ing my own daughter."

"She's going to make it," I say quietly.

"How can you be so sure?"

I hold up my hands. "I don't know. Maybe it's just a feeling. But I'm praying. A lot of people are praying ... I'm trying
to have faith."

She nods. "Faith comes more easily to some people."

"The Bible says faith is a gift from God. He'll give it to
anyone who asks."

She presses her lips together, as if she's stewing on this.

"I think the best way to help Fran right now is to keep
things very calm and peaceful around here. She needs rest.
And stress is very draining. In fact, I think it's toxic—for both
of you."

Mrs. Bishop has tears in her eyes now. "I'm just not good
in this kind of situation. I've never been a patient woman, and
I like to speak my mind."

"You're a strong person," I tell her. "But I think you need
to use your strength to build Fran up—not tear her down.
Instead of focusing on the negative, focus on the positive.
What can it hurt?"

She pulls a tissue out of her pocket, wiping her nose, and
nods. "I know you're right. That's what Fran's father used to
say ... before he passed."

"I think you're going to be fine." I smile. "But feel free to
call me if you need help. I'll be at my mom's house this afternoon, and I'll keep my cell on. The number's by the phone in
the kitchen."

"Thank you." She sniffs. "And I'm sorry for being so
cranky with you, Erin. I think in some ways I've been jealous."

"Jealous?"

"You seem like such a natural at caregiving, and yet you're so young … and here I am, *Fran's own mother*, and I'm bumbling around like a big-mouthed idiot."

"It's probably because you're so worried about her. I don't know how I'd feel if I were you … if I had a child who was ill like this."

"I'm so afraid for her. It feels as if it's eating me alive sometimes."

"I wish you could do what I do."

"What?" Her eyes are desperate, like a drowning person reaching for a life preserver. "Tell me!"

"I try to give my worries and fears to God." I sigh, knowing how often I fail. "It's not that I'm always successful at it. But I keep trying, because I know that when I trust God with all that stuff, it takes the load off me and I can relax a little. Plus I'm a nicer person to be around. But, believe me, I'm still learning to do this too. I blow it all the time."

She has a thoughtful look, as if she's trying to absorb this, then nods. "That's what I'll try to do too."

"Good." I pat her on the back. "I'll see you at the hospital tomorrow."

"I swear, I will really try to do better," she promises as I'm leaving. As I go, I pray she does.

Today is the first time that Mom and Jon have had Paige and me over for a meal. I can tell as soon as I'm in the house that Mom is a little nervous, like she wants everything to be picture perfect. I know how my mom is about meals—a perfectionist. It's like she always wants her table to look like a scene from a food magazine. I know it's pointless to attempt to convince her it doesn't matter, that a lunch should be about the people and not the food, or that it's okay if something is burnt or underdone.

"Smells good in here," I say when I come into the kitchen.

"Thanks. It's a new recipe." She chuckles as I give her a sideways hug. "You're not supposed to experiment with company. But you girls are family, so I guess it's okay."

"It looks interesting," I say while I survey the ingredients spread over the island. "What are you making?"

"Moroccan," she says as she chops something green. "Jon's been wanting me to try it." She points to an oddly shaped pot on the stove. "That's a tangine," she explains. "Kind of like a Moroccan slow cooker. We're having chicken tangine." She lists the ingredients, which are mostly spices.

"Exotic." I sneak a carrot. "Anything I can do to help?"

"Not really." She tosses the green stuff onto the carrots then wipes her hands. "Everything is pretty much ready to go; it's just a matter of time." She nods to the fridge. "Why don't you get yourself something to drink and join Paige and Jon out by the pool? I'll be along in a minute."

I grab some orange soda water and go out to where Jon and Paige are lounging in the shade. Fortunately the weather has finally cooled down. "Hey," I say as I pull up a lounger and stretch out. "What a day."

"Uh-huh . . ." Paige sighs contentedly.

"Paige was just telling me about her plans for New York." Jon chuckles. "Wish I could go too."

"What plans?" I ask.

"You know . . . for Eliza." Paige gives me a sly look.

"You mean you have a specific plan?"

"Not exactly specific," she admits. "Just some sweet revenge."

"You know what they say," Jon tells me. "Hell hath no fury like a woman scorned."

"What are you talking bout?" Mom asks as she joins us.

"Paige's plan to get even," Jon tells her.

"Even with whom?" Mom sits down at the end of Jon's lounger.

"Eliza Wilton," I tell her. "Who else?"

"What do you mean?" Mom turns to Paige. "You're not going to pull some crazy stunt in New York, are you?"

Paige makes her innocent face.

"Paige?" Mom looks concerned.

"What?" Paige frowns. "You're not suggesting I go to New York and treat Eliza like nothing happened, are you?"

"Actually, I am."

"Oh, Mom!" Paige makes a disgusted moan. "Don't go Goody Two-shoes on me now."

"I'm not going Goody Two-shoes," Mom protests. "I'm simply speaking as your director. You're a professional. You can't go to New York to seek revenge against Eliza Wilton."

"Why not?" Paige demands. "She's asked for it."

"For one thing, you don't even know what happened in the Bahamas. According to Dylan, it was—"

"Eliza bragged about it to me," Paige shoots back. "Right in the lobby of our hotel."

"She bragged that Dylan *spent the night*," Mom corrects. "And Dylan hasn't denied spending the night. The question is whether or not he actually cheated on you. And I don't think you know the answer to that yet."

Paige folds her arms in front of her, wearing the same

pouty face she used to make as a child when she didn't get her way.

"But think about it, Brynn," Jon says gently. "At the very least, Eliza tried to give Paige a bad impression about her fiancée. What kind of a girl does something like that?"

"A girl like Eliza Wilton," I say. "She is the most spoiled princess I've ever met."

"She seemed like a nice enough person to me," Mom says.

Paige's eyes flash. "You've got to be kidding!"

"Eliza conducted herself like a perfect lady on *Britain's Got Style*." Mom nods to Paige. "Meanwhile, Paige let the show down that day." She turns to Jon. "I didn't tell you she didn't make it because she was in her hotel room nursing a hangover."

Jon gives a mock *tsk-tsk* as he playfully shakes his finger at Paige.

"I didn't do it on purpose," Paige says defensively. "I felt perfectly horrible about the whole thing. And Erin did fine without me."

"You don't really know Eliza," I tell Mom. "She can be really nasty and mean. We've seen it. She's extremely competitive and will do almost anything to get her own way."

"And does that make it acceptable for Paige to go to New York—in the guise of doing your TV show—in order to wreak revenge on her?"

"That's not why we're going to New York," Paige protests. "We really are doing a show. And I can't help it that we'll cross paths with Eliza. After all, she *is* partnered with Rhiannon."

"Yes, I know you'll cross Eliza's path, Paige. But that doesn't mean you have to engage in some kind of ridiculous catfight."

Paige holds her head up. "I have no intention of engaging in a catfight, Mother."

"That's a relief." Mom looks at me. "I just want my girls to take the high road. You don't need to reduce yourselves to someone else's low standards."

"Are you saying that as our director or as our mother?" I ask.

Mom looks slightly stumped. "Both, I suppose."

I glance at Jon, and he looks a bit uncomfortable. "I know it's not really my business," he says gently, "but you might have to remove your mother hat while you're working for their show, Brynn."

"That's right," Paige says quickly. "If you make us act like perfect little ladies and our show turns into a total snooze, Helen will *not* be happy."

"Even Fran said she hopes we have cameras running when Paige confronts Eliza."

"Really?" Paige looks surprised.

"Of course, we don't have to use the footage, but we should film it just in case it's show-worthy. And in case you and Dylan really do break up, it might be good to show the reason why before the tabloids run amok with it."

"Run amok?" Paige giggles.

"You know what I mean."

"Well, I can see I'm in the minority here." Mom stands and puts her hands on her hips. "Maybe you girls would like someone else to produce and direct your show in New York."

"No, Mom," I insist. "That's not it at all."

Paige doesn't say anything.

"It's just that we need to understand each other," I explain quickly. "We have to be on the same page before we go to New York."

"I'll be curious to hear Helen's view on this," Mom responds as she heads back into the house.

"I know Helen's view," Paige says after Mom's gone. "And it has to do with the bottom line."

Not surprisingly, our Moroccan lunch is a relatively quiet and polite meal. We all try to smooth things over, but it's obvious Mom's feelings are hurt. And as I'm driving home, I think it must be difficult being a mom. Maybe it's especially hard for moms of daughters. It's like they identify with us too closely — they think what we do is a personal reflection on them. And yet we're just trying to be ourselves and live our own lives. I wonder if Mollie will go through this sort of thing with Fern some day — which is very weird to think about.

Chapter 7

Monday morning's meeting in Helen's office feels like we're picking up right where we left off yesterday. "I'm not sure I understand you, Brynn," Helen says to my mom. "Are you saying that you don't want to direct the show?"

Mom is frustrated and I feel sorry for her. "I'm saying I can't encourage my daughters to act like mean middle-school girls for the whole world to see—no matter how much the ratings would love it."

"And you think that's what I'm suggesting?" Helen looks offended.

"I think you're both saying the same thing," I interject. "But in different ways." Now all eyes are on me and I know I need to explain. "It's the same as always," I say to Helen. "You want Paige and me to mind our manners—as well as to be ourselves and get a good show. Right?"

Helen nods. "Right."

"That's what I want too," Mom says a bit meekly.

"Except that you want to control us," Paige points out.

"No . . . not really."

"Look, Brynn." Helen adjusts her glasses. "This is not Channel Five News. Your job is not to control anything. Your job is to keep things rolling, keep people doing what they're hired to do, and to just let things happen. The best reality TV directors know how to step back." She peers at Mom. "Do you know how to step back?"

Mom frowns. "I'll admit that's not easy when we're talking about my own daughters."

"We're your daughters," Paige says, "but you don't own us."

"I never said I did."

"But that's what it feels like when you talk like that."

"Well, I'm sorry." Mom folds her arms.

"And, see . . ." Paige stands and holds out her hands. "This is exactly what I've always been afraid of. I mean, if Mom directs, it could turn into a mother-daughter power struggle."

"That's not what we want." Helen rocks a pen between her fingers with a stumped expression.

The room has become so quiet, you can feel it.

"I guess I should step down then," Mom says sadly.

"Maybe so . . ." Helen sets the pen on her desk. "I suppose I should've considered this possibility before. It just seemed so handy, and rather sweet—a mother and her daughters doing a show together. But maybe it's unrealistic." She laughs uneasily. "Or maybe it's just an entirely different reality show."

Mom looks at me. "So did it feel awkward like this to you in the Bahamas?" She turns to Paige. "Or to you?"

"No," I tell her. "I thought you did a great job of jumping into Fran's role."

"I did too," Paige admits. "But it's like you've changed since then . . . like you've got some kind of ownership thing going on. I'm not sure if it's because we're your daughters or you're just taking the responsibility of producing and directing too seriously."

Mom frowns. "Well, producing the news was always rather serious."

"And perhaps you're unable to take the news hat off," Helen tells her. "Not everyone can do reality TV, Brynn. Take it from me, I know from experience. You're either cut out for it or you're not."

Mom sighs. "Well, I'm not sure. I did enjoy working with the girls in the Bahamas. And I'd like another chance to prove myself." She stands and faces Paige. "But I'll understand if you'd rather have someone else."

"Oh, Mom." Paige looks like she's about to cry. "I would like you to come. It's just that I don't want you to take over."

"I know." Mom nods. "And I think I can learn how to keep my mouth shut."

"Unless you see us doing something really crazy," I tell her.

"Fran always knew when to reel us back," Paige says. "But she did it gently and professionally."

"Right." Mom nods.

"And not because we were embarrassing her either," Paige adds.

"Well, you don't want to embarrass yourselves, do you?"

Suddenly Paige and Mom are starting to go at it again, so I hold up my hands. "I know this meeting needs to end at ten," I say more to Helen than anyone.

"That's right." Helen nods to the clock on the wall.

"And this afternoon is Fran's transplant, so I thought maybe we could give her a minute or so of our thoughts and prayers. Is that okay, Helen?"

"It's perfect. Let's do it."

And so the room gets quiet again, but this time it's not a harsh sort of silence. I can tell that everyone's changed focus now. I pray silently and after a couple of minutes, Helen actually says, "amen."

Helen stands, gathers some things from her desk, and slips them into her briefcase. "I'm going to let you ladies sort this out. Just let me know if we need to track down another director. And, if so, I want to know by four o'clock sharp. Good day!" With that, she is gone.

"So . . ." Paige purses her lips like she's thinking.

"So . . . I think you girls should make the decision without me." Mom picks up her purse. "All I have to say is that *if* you decide you want me to come, I will try to direct the show the way I think Fran would. I can't promise that it'll go perfectly smoothly, but I promise I'll try to be less of a mother and more of a coworker." She slips out of the room.

Then it's just Paige and me, still sitting in Helen's executive office. "So," I begin, "what do *you* want to do?"

"You're going to make me decide?" Paige scowls. "So I can be the bad guy?"

"No, I'm not trying to put it all on you. I just think we need to discuss this."

"It's such a mess," she grumbles.

"I know . . . and I feel sad for Mom."

"Me too." Paige sighs as she sits back down.

"What do we do?"

Her mouth twists to one side, like she's thinking hard.

Suddenly I'm curious. "Also, I want to know if you have a specific plan for Eliza. I mean, you wouldn't do anything seriously messed up, would you?"

"Of course not." And yet her smile is mischievous.

"I mean you wouldn't embarrass yourself or the show, would you?"

"You know I wouldn't."

I nod. "Okay, I realize you wouldn't risk your own image. But you do understand that if you push something too far with Eliza, it will make you look bad?"

"I'm not an idiot, Erin." Her voice is growing colder.

"And you heard Helen's warning about lawsuits. The Wilton family could afford to drag us and the entire network through the court system until you and I are old enough to retire."

Her brow creases. "I'll keep that in mind."

I'm hopeful I can trust Paige. If nothing else, she loves her public image enough to watch her step. "So—back to Mom."

"Okay. Let's give her a chance."

I stare at my sister. "*Really?* You're good with that?"

"Sure. If she messes up, we can always let her go before the Milan trip."

"Yeah … right." I'm imagining the tabloid headlines— "Forrester Sisters Fire Mom."

"She'll probably be just fine." Paige stands like we're done. "Mom heard Helen spell it out, and she's not dumb. She has to understand that this is different than news TV. And, really, she wasn't too bad in the Bahamas."

"I'll try to help her as much as I can," I offer.

Paige sticks out her hand. "So we agree this is the right thing to do."

"We agree." We shake hands and, as we leave Helen's office, I'm hoping we won't be sorry.

"I'll call Mom," Paige offers as we go outside. She barely has her phone out when she lets out a squawk.

"What's wrong?"

She holds her phone in my face. "Look at this!"

I cup my hand over the small screen to see what looks like a photo of Paige and Ben. "Is that from Saturday night?"

"Yes." She lets out a growl. "Mollie forwarded it to me. She says it's all over the place. Listen to this headline. 'Paige Forrester Breaks Engagement for Benjamin Kross?' Can you believe that? It's like they can say anything they want as long as they put a question mark at the end of the lie."

"Hopefully people see the question mark as a reason to question the accuracy of the headline," I tell her as we stop by her car.

"I know it's not worth getting upset over." Paige takes a deep breath. "And, in a way, I don't even care. In fact, I'm curious to hear Dylan's reaction."

"Does he follow the tabloid garbage?"

"No, but I'm sure some of his employees do. He'll hear about it soon enough."

"And you don't plan to do damage control first?"

She shrugs. "Nope."

I'm tempted to point out that this seems a bit immature on her part. But, come to think of it, her whole relationship with Dylan seems a bit juvenile, especially thanks to the Eliza episode. It's childish behavior for a couple who are supposedly engaged. I hope if I ever get engaged—and I'm not planning anything soon—I'll handle myself with a bit more class.

Paige and I part ways and I drive over to Cedars-Sinai, where I find Fran's mother in the waiting area of the oncology unit. "Fran just went in," Mrs. Bishop informs me as she sets aside a rumpled magazine. "I think she's calmer about this whole thing than I am."

"You know, the procedure is actually fairly simple," I remind her. "At least for the recipient. It's more of an ordeal for the donor."

"Yes." Mrs. Bishop nods. "We met the donor last week. He seems like a fine, healthy man. And we heard he went through the surgery this morning with no problems."

"Good."

"I'm trying to focus on the positives," she says. "It's not easy, especially when I remember all the things that can still go wrong. There's a long list of possible complications, Erin. Fran could get hit with anything from a severe infection to kidney failure — and even if she escapes those troubles, there's no guarantee that she'll be cancer-free." She lets out a jagged sigh.

"I know, but I'm trying *not* to think about those things." Then to distract her, I tell her about our moment of prayerful silence at work. I also rattle on about the meeting this morning and how my mom is having a hard time fitting into Fran's shoes. "I'm not sure if it's because of her experience producing the news or because of Paige and me."

Her voice sounds shrill. "I cannot, for the life of me, imagine working with my daughter. I'm sure we would fight constantly. It's hard enough trying to live with her."

I have to bite my tongue, because I'm pretty sure it's Fran's mom who's hard to live with. But I could be wrong.

The procedure is supposed to take about three hours and it's nearly two o'clock when I hear my stomach growling. I offer to get some lunch for us. Mrs. Bishop says she's not hungry, but I tell her I'll try to find something to tempt her. Then, on my way to the cafeteria, I check my phone. There's a message from my mom, asking me to call her.

"Hey, Mom," I say cheerfully. "What's up?"

"Paige says you girls decided to give me another chance."

"Oh, it's not really like that," I say. "We both know you'd be really good at directing, Mom. And as long as we can avoid the mother-daughter conflicts, we should be okay. Don't you think?"

"I hope so, Erin." Then she asks if I saw the photo of Ben and Paige.

"Yeah." I get into line at the cafeteria. "Paige didn't seem too concerned though."

"She *should* be concerned."

"I kind of felt like that at first too, but then I wondered what good it does to react at all. You know how it goes—the tabloids are going to print whatever they think will grab some attention. And that little blurb about Paige and Ben will blow over as soon as a bigger celeb does something sensational."

"Yes, I suppose you're right."

"So are you glad you're coming to New York with us?" I ask hopefully.

"I guess so ... but I'm a little uneasy too."

"You'll be fine, Mom. You know, I was starting to help Fran some, and doing some interning to learn the inside part of the business. Maybe I can help you too."

"That would be nice. Paige wants to have a planning meeting tomorrow morning at the studio. She said Leah will be on hand to help too. Hopefully I can muddle through somehow." Then she changes topics by asking about Fran.

"The procedure must be about midway through," I tell her. "Fran's mom is pretty nervous. In fact, I was just getting us some lunch."

"I won't keep you then. Tell Fran I'm sending positive thoughts her way."

"I'll let her know."

I return to the waiting area with two different soups and salads. To my relief, Mrs. Bishop discovers she has an appetite after all. Eating helps to pass the time, but then we're back at the waiting game again. I start feeling anxious, so I excuse myself to dispose of our lunch remainders and then, on my way back, stop in a quiet corner to pray for Fran. I also pray for the donor.

At half past three, the doctor comes to the waiting room to tell us that the procedure is finished and that Fran is doing well and resting.

"So it went well?" Mrs. Bishop asks nervously.

"As well as it could possibly go," the doctor tells her.

"And do you really think she should go home?" she asks. "Today?"

The doctor nods. "Yes. Fran has made it clear she prefers to recover at home. And because her apartment is so close to the hospital, I don't think there's any need for concern." She hands Mrs. Bishop a packet of papers. "Fran understands the need to be very germ-conscious during this time, as I'm sure you do as well, but here's some information to help you care for her. Do you have any questions?"

"I guess not." She looks down at the papers in her hand.

"Feel free to call the number there if you do."

"When can we see her?" Mrs. Bishop asks.

"I'd like her to rest quietly for about an hour. Then we'll check her vitals." The doctor smiles. "If everything is okay, she can be released around six."

To celebrate, Mrs. Bishop and I go get a cup of coffee. "Thank you so much for waiting with me today," she says as we head back up to see Fran. "You have no idea how much it means to me."

"Well, Fran is a special person," I tell her. "I feel like I've been through so much with her already. How could I not come?"

When we find Fran later, she looks tired but relieved. I tell her how everyone is sending warm wishes her way and we visit a bit. There's a new light in her eyes, but it's plain she still needs some rest.

And although I know it will be some time before the transplant really begins to reverse her leukemia, I still feel very hopeful as I drive home. I believe Fran is going to make it!

Chapter
8

On Thursday morning a town car, arranged by Leah, picks us up to go to the airport. Mom's already in the back with her laptop open, going over some of the details as we ride to LAX. *So far, so good*, I'm thinking as we get out, gather up our bags, and head inside. Paige is wearing oversized sunglasses with her hair tucked into a hat. I'm not sure about her attempt to go incognito, since I know from experience that this getup attracts nearly as much attention as her usual look. However, it's either a slow day at LAX or the paparazzi have already found someone else to chase, because our entrance into the terminal is uneventful.

"Remember when Paige got tackled by security?" I say quietly to Mom as we're checking our bags.

Mom chuckles. "Don't remind me."

"Well, she's been very careful ever since." I smile at my sister as she hands her luggage over. She gave up her Pepto-Bismol pink bags months ago, but her Louis Vuitton is fairly easy to spot—and if you ask me, more tempting to steal. Paige no longer seems too worried about that, however.

After we're settled at our gate, Paige and I get some magazines and things. As I'm browsing a photography magazine, I hear my sister make a little yelp. She's standing by the gossip rags, and I figure she's seen another tidbit about herself and Ben, but she holds up a tabloid with a photo of Eliza and Dylan. The headline says "Heiress Steals Paige Forrester's Man." And this time there is no question mark.

I go over and examine the picture. "That looks like an old photo," I tell Paige. "And it looks like it's been tampered with." I shrug. "No surprises there."

"But listen to this," Paige says angrily. "'Eliza Wilton confesses to a secret tryst with designer Dylan Marceau during Bahamas Fashion Week. Marceau is engaged to fashionista Paige Forrester, star of the popular TV series *On the Runway*, but their relationship is reported to be on the rocks.'" She reads a little more then throws the paper down. "Disgusting!"

Several girls cluster nearby, whispering. It's obvious they recognize us.

"Come on," I urge Paige. "They're probably pre-boarding our flight by now." We make our purchases and, realizing that I'm as uninterested in publicity as Paige is, I follow her lead and don shades before we rejoin Mom. Meanwhile Paige stands by a post with her head down, focused on her iPhone, probably checking out the rumor mills to see who is saying what about her and Dylan and Eliza.

I tell Mom about the tabloid and she just shakes her head. "There ought to be a law." Then she laughs. "Oh, yeah, there is. But it's pretty hard to prove slander in a court of law. Especially for celebrities."

"It's funny, isn't it?" I say. "Paige being a celebrity. It's like I sometimes forget—you know, when we're just hanging out at home, doing normal stuff. And then we're out in public and something happens and it's like — wow, she really is famous."

"So are you," Mom tells me.

I laugh and adjust my sunglasses. "Yeah, right. The only reason I put these on was to disguise the fact that I'm Paige's sister."

"So do you think this is going to ratchet up her little revenge plan?" Mom glances nervously at Paige. "I know I promised to hold back, but I can't let her do anything too ir-responsible, can I?"

"No, of course not. It's not like we want her to end up in jail or court." I hold up my phone. "And that reminds me. I asked Fran about being our phone-a-friend."

"Phone-a-friend?"

"Yeah, kind of an absentee consultant. She said it's okay for you to call or email her with questions. And if she's up to it, she'll advise you."

"That's sweet. How's she doing, anyway?"

"She says she feels stronger every day. I think part of it is just the relief of having the transplant behind her now, because it's probably too early for real results." I email my mom Fran's phone number and email address. "There, you can reach her whenever you want to now."

"I don't want to disturb her."

"Then just email or text her. She can decide whether or not to respond." I pause to hear the PA announcement. "Looks like we can load now."

"That was for first class."

I grin at her. "I know."

She laughs then reaches for her carry-on. "Oh, I forgot."

Soon we're seated, but Paige is still glued to her iPhone.

I can tell by her expression the news is not good. "How's it going?" I ask.

"I want to kill her."

"When did she say all this anyway?"

"In an interview with *Couture* magazine. At least that's what they seem to be quoting from. But the magazine hasn't even hit the newsstands yet, so apparently there's a mole somewhere."

"Why would *Couture* even want to interview Eliza in the first place?"

"Because of her partnership with Rhiannon. And don't forget that Katherine Carter mentored both of those girls, and she still has deep connections with that magazine."

"That's true."

"There can only be one reason Eliza is saying this stuff."

"What?"

"She's trying to get Dylan."

"Seems to me it'd be hard to get anyone who didn't want to be gotten."

Paige frowns and actually looks close to tears.

"Sorry, I didn't mean it like that. I meant that Eliza can do all kinds of crazy stuff, but if Dylan isn't into her, what's the worry?"

Paige just shrugs, tossing her phone into her bag.

"Is it possible they got the Eliza quotes wrong?" I ask. "I mean, consider the source. How often do they get this stuff right?"

"I suppose that's a possibility. But usually there's a grain of truth in their stories. Even if it is twisted."

"The truth is probably that Eliza *wishes* she could get Dylan."

Ciao!

Paige opens her fashion magazine, flipping through the pages so quickly, I'm sure she's not even looking. I have nothing more to say, so I pull my book from my bag. I started Jane Austen's *Pride and Prejudice* a couple of days ago and, although the book was written two centuries ago, I'm surprised at how relevant it still is today. In fact, in some ways the two older sisters—Jane and Elizabeth—remind me of Paige and me. Well, except that Jane (the pretty sister and the one who would be Paige) is quite shy. My sister is anything but shy.

It's a little past six when we collect our bags in JFK, and we're on our way to our town car when Paige stops in her tracks, pointing toward the doors. And there is Dylan, waving at her.

"Did you know he was meeting your flight?" Mom asks her.

"No." Paige looks uncertain. "What do I do?"

"It's up to you," Mom says calmly.

When we reach the doors, Dylan is smiling. "I have a cab waiting," he tells Paige.

"Our town car is already here," Paige replies in a snooty tone.

His disappointment is obvious. "Oh ..."

Mom and I exchange stilted greetings with him as we make our way out to the crowded sidewalk, where passengers are securing transportation. I wave to the driver who is holding a sign that says *Forrester*. "There's our ride," I tell Mom. Meanwhile Dylan just stands with his hands in his pockets, looking at Paige with sad eyes. I can't help but feel sorry for him. He looks so clueless.

"Let me help with that." Dylan grabs the luggage cart from me. The next thing we know, he's helping our driver load our bags into the trunk of the town car. Paige is just getting in the car when Dylan stops her, grabbing her by the hand. "Can I take you to dinner?" he asks hopefully. "I made reservations at Babbo—"

"We need to talk," she says in a chilly voice.

"I know." He glances at Mom and me uncomfortably.

Mom and I get into the back of the car, and Mom closes the door to give them privacy. "Don't leave yet," she tells the driver. "Give us a couple more minutes."

"This is so awkward," I whisper. Mom just nods. Then we sit and try not to stare as Dylan and Paige exchange words.

Finally Paige opens the door. "I guess I'm going with him," she says in a grumpy voice.

"Are you sure?" I ask. "You know you don't have to go if you don't want to."

She shrugs. "No, it's okay. I want to. We might as well hash it all out." She makes a smirk. "Besides it's *Babbo*. How can I resist?"

"Have *fun*," I say in a teasing tone.

"Don't be out too late," Mom warns. Then she smiles. "Remember we have the interview with Rhiannon in the morning. And morning comes early on East-Coast time."

"Yeah, yeah." Paige nods and waves. "Don't worry. I won't be out late."

Mom tells the driver we're ready to leave and confirms which hotel we're going to. I think that this isn't all that different from how Fran would handle things.

"Ah, New York," Mom sighs. "If you'd told me three weeks ago that I'd be here today I wouldn't have believed it."

"So you're not sorry you quit Channel Five?" I ask.

She laughs. "Not even a little. I didn't realize until my last day how much stress was tied up in that job."

"This one's not exactly stress-free," I remind her.

"Yes, but it's a different kind of stress. It's stress with benefits."

"Right …" I look out to where the traffic has come to a complete standstill. "So, what do you think about Paige and Dylan?"

She shrugs. "I have no idea what to think. I just hope Paige gets to the bottom of this. If Dylan is truly innocent, it seems cruel to make him suffer."

"Do *you* think he's innocent?"

Mom frowns. "I'm not sure. At first I thought he wasn't. But he's made such an effort to win Paige back. I honestly don't know."

We eventually make it to our hotel. I had expected New York to be less busy since it's not Fashion Week, but the city is a beehive of activity. After we're checked in and somewhat unpacked, Mom and I decide to see if we can find a restaurant within walking distance. The concierge makes a couple of calls and it's a little before nine when we're seated in a French bistro only a block away. The food is excellent and Mom even orders a glass of wine.

As we eat, we compare notes on Paris. All in all it's a fun evening, and although Mom feels a bit sad that Paige isn't here, I enjoy having my mom to myself for a change.

Afterward, as we're going into the hotel lobby, we spy Dylan and Paige sitting with their heads bent together in the hotel lounge.

"She'd better not be drinking," Mom says sharply.

I peer closely and see that Paige has a cup and saucer in front of her. "I think it's just coffee," I assure Mom.

"Good."

When we get to our rooms—Paige and I are sharing a suite that's adjoined to Mom's room—I promise to keep tabs on Paige and make sure she gets to bed on time. I also think this is a way to make sure Dylan doesn't spend the night. Not that I think that's likely, considering the past few weeks … but with my sister, you never know.

"I'll check in with the crew," Mom says as she unlocks her door, "and I'll make sure they're all set to meet us at the design studio tomorrow." We're operating with a small crew for this trip. Luis is here to do hair, but Paige will be in charge of our makeup. And we only have two camera guys, JJ and Alistair. I think, for Mom's sake, this is probably fortunate. There's less to manage.

It's just a bit past eleven when Paige makes her appearance. "We're bunking together?" she asks as she tosses her bag onto a chair by the door.

"Yeah, it was Mom or me," I tell her. "I'm willing to use the sleeper sofa if you want the bed to yourself."

She peeks into the bedroom. "No, that's okay. It's a king and you don't usually snore … too loudly."

"Very funny."

She kicks off her shoes and zips open a garment bag, humming as if she's perfectly content and the world is once again her oyster.

"So, how did it go with Dylan?"

"Okay."

"Just okay?"

"Well, we talked a lot, and I guess I'm starting to believe him about Eliza."

"Meaning that she really is making the whole thing up?"

Paige nods as she pulls out a linen suit and gives it a shake. "Guess this is going to need to be pressed before morning." She frowns at the clock. "Probably too late to have it done."

"Probably." I go to the closet and pull out the ironing board and get it set up. I'm fully aware that my sister can iron her own clothes, but I'm also aware that it'll be easier in the long run if I do it.

"It'll need steam," she says as I'm about to plug in the iron.

I take the iron to the kitchenette, fill it with water (hoping she doesn't complain that it's from the tap), then return and plug it in. "So what does Dylan say about Eliza making those statements to the press about him?"

"He thinks she's been misquoted." She hangs up some other clothing, artfully arranging them in order of garment and color, about an inch apart on the closet rod—like she thinks someone is going to photograph it.

"What do you think?" I ask.

"I'm not sure."

"Well, do you believe Dylan? I mean that he didn't cheat on you?"

She turns to me with her lips pressed together and brow creased. "I *think* I believe him."

"But you're not one hundred percent positive?"

"Maybe eighty percent."

I get the linen suit, taking it off the hanger, and begin to steam it. It's Michael Kors and a very nice cut. I know Paige will look classy in it. Totally Grace Kelly.

"What am I wearing tomorrow?" I ask as she starts unpacking another bag. Although Leah helped pack things, Paige is entirely in charge of wardrobe for this trip.

"How about this?" She holds up a pale blue suit, also in linen. "It's Ralph Lauren. It looks light and summery and I think it'll go well with my suit."

"It's pretty," I admit. "Sure you don't want to wear it? That blue would look great with your eyes."

"It's *your* size, Erin."

"Oh." I nod. "I'll press it too."

She's going through shoes now, choosing what we'll wear with the suits and setting them out, along with accessories, so that our outfits are all ready to go in the morning. I'm always amazed at how easily she does this. She's like a style magician. She does it so effortlessly, almost as if she's playing Barbies. She tries this and that and then quickly decides—but once it's all in place, it's perfect. I'll admit it's taken me awhile, but I've learned not to question her fashion sense.

"So… if we see Eliza tomorrow," I begin cautiously, "how are you going to act?"

She makes that mischievous little smile. "I'm not sure."

"I thought you had some kind of plan."

She shrugs. "Maybe … maybe not. I think I'll just see how it plays out."

"And maybe she won't even be there," I say hopefully.

"Maybe not."

Before long, the suits are steamed, and while I'm taking a shower Paige goes to bed. I set the alarm for eight, which is about when Luis is supposed to get here, and go to bed too. I feel slightly apprehensive about tomorrow's interview with Rhiannon. I'm hoping perhaps Eliza will make herself scarce. It would seem the wise route to take, considering.

But, just in case she doesn't, I decide to pray specifically. I ask God to help Paige not to do anything regrettable. I ask

God to help my mom do her job to the best of her ability. And then I ask God to use me as a buffer if needed. I hope I'm dead wrong, but I believe that tomorrow has the potential to go totally sideways on all of us.

Chapter 9

Despite the heat radiating from the pavement of the city, which never cooled off last night, Paige seems cool and calm as we get into the town car. She seems not to have a care in the world as we ride to Rhiannon's design studio.

"You girls both look lovely," Mom tells us as we get out of the car. Paige smoothes the front of her skirt, which didn't even wrinkle, unlike mine. How does she do that?

"Looks like it's showtime," I say as I spot Alistair waiting by the door with a ready camera.

"Then JJ should be inside," Mom informs us. "Take it away."

"Here we are at Rhiannon Farley's new design studio," Paige says into the hand mic she's using. "Very uptown and chic." She glances up at the sleek building. "And no doubt expensive."

We go inside and, instead of being greeted by an assistant like we usually are when it's a big-name designer, we are met by Rhiannon herself. "Welcome," she says happily. "Thank you so much for coming."

JJ's camera is running too as we exchange greetings and Rhiannon shows us around the spacious showroom, holding up some of her recent designs.

"These are for my spring line," she says as she waves to a rack. "I'm calling it Linen and Lace." She smiles at our linen suits. "Kind of like what you're wearing, only a bit more feminine and Old World. The lace is all recycled and the linen is organic." She continues, showing us pieces and explaining some of the thought behind her designs.

"And I hear you just landed a new account," Paige says cheerfully.

"Yes!" Rhiannon claps her hands. "One of my very favorite stores too. Anthropologie is trying out some of my garments. I'm so excited."

"Congratulations," I tell her. "I love Anthropologie as well."

"They'll be in the winter catalog."

"I'll be watching," I say.

"So come on into the design room," she says as she leads us down a hallway. "This is where it all happens." As she shows us a room that's filled with everything from burlap sacks to beaded bags to old buttons, it's obvious that this is not the typical designer's workspace.

"So let's pretend you're starting a new design," Paige says to her. "Where would you begin?"

Rhiannon starts looking around, gathering up some pieces that I can't really imagine working together. She picks up a drawing pad and starts to sketch. Then she's laying things out. And then she explains the garment she's creating, showing us her drawing and which materials go where—and it's like a light goes on. I get it.

"Wow," I say. "You could take those items and turn them into that?"

She laughs. "Hopefully. It takes help from my crew. I can't believe how cool it is to have real seamstresses working under me. I was so used to doing everything myself. To be honest, it was a little hard to let go at first. But now that I'm used to it, all I want to do is design and design."

"You're very young to be a designer on her own," Paige points out.

Rhiannon nods. "And I'm not too proud to admit that has a lot to do with some excellent connections." She talks about how Katherine Carter mentored her and how she introduced Rhiannon to some important people in the fashion world. "But I really owe this studio to my new partner, Eliza Wilton." Now Rhiannon looks slightly uncomfortable, as if she is aware of the rumors swirling about her business associate.

"Yes, I know that Ms. Wilton used to do some professional modeling and has some fashion experience, but how involved is she in the actual design process?" Paige asks with surprising ease.

"Eliza primarily handles the business end of things." Rhiannon pauses. "Although she sometimes gives me input." She laughs nervously. "Not that I always take it. Our senses of style are quite different. In fact, some have questioned how we can actually work together as a team. But so far it seems to be going well, and I'm hugely appreciative of this partnership. I know I wouldn't be where I am today without Eliza."

I'm thinking she really means "without Eliza's money," but I would never say this.

"Is it possible to get a few words with Ms. Wilton?" Paige asks. "Some of our viewers might be interested to learn a bit about the business perspective of a design firm."

"Sure." Rhiannon moves toward the door, with cameras trailing. "Let's go see if she's in her office."

As we go down the hall again, I feel certain that Eliza will not be in her office today. Really, why would she set herself up for this? But when Rhiannon knocks, Eliza answers. "Yes?"

"Surprise!" Paige sings out.

Eliza's blue eyes grow wide and it's obvious she's been caught totally off guard. Suddenly I wonder if she even knew that our show was coming to New York to film. Is it possible she was kept in the dark? What if Rhiannon didn't want Eliza to know—wanted to keep a lid on things? But then why would she have knocked on the door?

"Do you mind if we get some words from you for our TV show, *On the Runway*?" Paige asks pleasantly. "I know some of our viewers will find it fascinating to hear about your role in the fashion industry. Because we know it takes all kinds of talents to create a successful line."

"I . . . uh . . ." Eliza glances from Paige to Rhiannon.

"Unless you're too busy," Paige says lightly.

"Oh, she's not *that* busy." Rhiannon enters the office. She goes to Eliza's desk, picking up an opened magazine in a teasing way.

"Fantastic!" Paige gently pushes her way into the modern-yet-elegant office too. It's obvious that a lot of money and probably an interior designer were involved in the setup of this sleek space. And I feel just slightly intrusive as we all string in after Paige, finding places among the contemporary pieces of furniture. Mom finds a corner as JJ mics Eliza, who sits at her desk, looking more and more uncomfortable. Rhiannon and I position ourselves in front of a cabinet near the desk.

After we're all situated, Paige takes a chair opposite Eliza.

"Now tell us about your regular workday, Eliza. How do you spend most of your time?"

"Well, I ... I oversee the bookkeepers and I, uh, I do a little research ..."

"Does your work keep you pretty busy?" Paige asks brightly.

Eliza looks truly uncomfortable now. I think I see beads of sweat on her forehead. "Busy enough."

"Because you know what our grandmothers would say," Paige continues in a perky tone.

"What's that?"

"Oh, you know the old saying about how *idle hands are the devil's workshop.*" Paige's smile seems genuine, but her blue eyes are like steel. "In your regular workday, I assume you handle publicity releases for Rhiannon too? And you probably do interviews for magazines and newspapers and whatnot?"

Eliza shrugs. "Sometimes I do."

"In fact, I think I recently saw something about you in the news ..." Paige puts a finger alongside her chin like she's thinking some diabolical thought. "Let's see, the article had to do with another designer ... I don't recall the name."

The office is silent.

"Perhaps *you* remember?" Paige leans toward Eliza.

Eliza's features get a hardened look, and I imagine I can see the wheels spinning in her head, like she's conjuring up some kind of escape route or defense plan.

"Oh," Eliza says innocently. "You must mean that drivel they're printing about Dylan and me." She laughs. "That's old news, Paige. The photo was probably from last year. Everyone knows Dylan and I have been good friends for ages."

Paige swings her forefinger in the air dramatically. "No,

no ... that's not quite what I read. The piece I read suggested that you and Dylan Marceau were much more than *just good friends*. I believe you were quoted as saying that—"

"Surely you know how unreliable tabloid quotes are," Eliza interrupts. "Anyone who believes that nonsense deserves to be duped."

Mom and I exchange fast glances and I can tell she's trying to decide how best to "direct" this. I give her a quick nervous smile, as if to say, *it's okay ... let it go ... we can cut later if necessary*. She barely tips her head in a nod.

"So are you saying that you haven't been romantically involved with Dylan Marceau?" Paige's expression is dead serious, as if she's suddenly turned into a prosecuting attorney. "Are you saying that you haven't been having an affair with him? Do you claim that all those rumors are simply that—*rumors*?"

Eliza shrugs, but her lips curl into an icy smile. "Really, Paige, your questions seem a bit out there. Tell me, is this business now, or is this personal? Because I do not see how my relationship with Dylan Marceau has anything to do with your little TV show."

"Oh, but it does, Eliza. This is *hot fashion news*. My viewers know that I'm engaged to *the famous designer* Dylan Marceau and they will be very interested to hear whether or not the gossip sheets are reporting the truth. Please, Eliza, set us all straight. Have you been sleeping with my fiancée?"

Eliza snaps her fingers toward the cameras. "Turn those off. Right now, before I call security."

"But we were invited here." Paige turns to Rhiannon, who looks slightly blindsided. "Right?"

Rhiannon nods, her eyes worried.

"And my show would like to get to the truth in this matter, Eliza. Please, for the record, set us straight. Are the tabloids right? Have you been having an affair with my fiancée?"

Eliza glares at Paige—looking as if she's tempted to pick up her silver letter opener and slit my sister's throat. I wonder if I should remove the potential weapon, but Eliza doesn't move and her lips seem to be sealed. I'm afraid this has turned into a standoff.

"Shall I take your silence to mean that it's true then?" Paige asks in a sad tone. "That you really did go after Dylan? You pursued him knowing full well that he was engaged?" She shakes her head. "I honestly hoped you had more character than that, Eliza."

Eliza suddenly gets a smug look, like she thinks she's won this round—or perhaps the whole match. "Seriously, Paige, I hardly see how it reflects on *my* character if Dylan prefers me to you. Perhaps you just need to cut your losses and move on."

Paige seems to be at a loss for words, which is unusual.

"Think of it this way," Eliza continues in a self-satisfied way. "At least you weren't married yet. In a way, you really should thank me."

"So you admit that you slept with Dylan in the Bahamas?" Paige demands point blank. "You don't deny it?"

"I neither confirm nor deny it. And I'm sure it's quite troubling to you, Paige, but really, *it's not public business.*"

Paige glances at me with a puzzled expression, almost as if she wants me to give her an answer, but I'm literally gape-mouthed now, waiting for her next move—and hoping she has one.

Paige turns back to Eliza. "You say your personal affairs

are not public business, Eliza, and yet you've helped thrust this into the public eye."

Eliza actually smiles now. "Well, you know what they say about publicity."

"I do know. And I happen to know something else about your life that's not public business, Eliza. At first I thought it was random, but in some ways it helps to explain how you've acted toward Dylan."

"What are you talking about?" Eliza narrows her eyes.

"There was another time you entered into an impulsive relationship with a fairly well-known man. Another time when you showed a lack of discretion, Eliza."

"What?" Eliza stands up, her chair flying backward.

"I'm talking about a little episode that occurred in the south of France. Your family tried to keep the story quiet, but I found—"

Eliza's face has paled considerably. "Turn off the cameras," she seethes.

"Why?" Paige asks innocently. "I thought you appreciated publicity?"

"Turn off the cameras," Eliza repeats in a flat tone.

Paige looks like she's considering Eliza's request and then she turns to JJ and Alistair. "Yes, please, do turn them off, guys."

JJ and Alistair look seriously reluctant, but Mom waves her hand at them. "Turn them off, boys. *Cut.*"

They lower the cameras and we all wait.

"What do you want?" Eliza asks quietly.

"The truth," Paige tells her.

"About Cannes?" Eliza looks scared.

"No ... I already know about Cannes, Eliza. I want the

truth about the Bahamas—and Dylan. Not for the show, but for me. I want to know what really happened."

With a dark scowl, Eliza folds her arms in front of her. *"Nothing happened!"*

Paige looks skeptical. "Really? Nothing happened between you and Dylan? Are you saying that when he stayed in your room during the hurricane *nothing happened*?"

"That's right. *Nothing* happened."

"Then why didn't you just say that from the beginning? Why have you dragged us all through this muck and mire and innuendo?"

She shrugs.

Paige seems stumped—or maybe she's just finished. She looks at me now, like she hopes I might have some brilliant idea or a way to wrap this up. And suddenly I do.

"Eliza?" I step closer. "How about if you say the same thing for the cameras now?"

"Forget it."

"No, listen." I use a coaxing tone. "Right now you look like a total skank in the public eye. Paige's fans are going to hate you. The fashion industry is going to suspect your integrity. If you have any self-respect at all, you should *want* for people to know the truth. Do you really want everyone thinking you tried to steal someone else's fiancée?"

"She's right," Rhiannon confirms. "Not only that, but your image is important to our business. You need to be honest, Eliza—for everyone's sake."

"Fine." Eliza tosses the camera guys an aggravated look. "Go ahead and turn your cameras on." She points to Paige. "Do not bring up Cannes."

"I don't plan to. In fact, I'll ask for that part to be edited out."

"Really?" Eliza looks skeptical.

"I'm not trying to humiliate you," Paige says evenly. "I only want the truth."

With cameras running, Paige questions Eliza—a bit more gently this time—and Eliza comes fairly clean as she relays her story.

"The hurricane was blowing pretty strong by late afternoon," she says. "I wanted to pick something up on the other side of the island, and I convinced Dylan to come with me. Of course, by the time we got to the hotel, the hurricane was in full force. So I asked Dylan to wait it out with me. Really, it wasn't safe to drive, and all public transportation was shut down by then."

"And you just happened to have a room at this particular hotel?" Paige asks. "During Fashion Week, when all the hotels were solidly booked?"

Eliza makes a catty smile. "My parents have a timeshare there."

"Handy," I say from the sidelines.

"Anyway, we went up to the suite to watch the storm," she continues. "And that was all that happened. I eventually went to bed. Dylan fell asleep on the sofa. He must've left sometime in the middle of the night, probably after the storm passed, because he was gone in the morning. End of story."

"So Dylan told me the truth right from the start." Paige shakes her head. "And this whole media frenzy was, as usual, much ado about nothing?"

"I wouldn't say *nothing*," I add. "Don't forget that the gossip rags usually get a fragment of their story from *some* source, whether it's accurate or not." I look at Eliza, but she just shrugs like she's innocent.

Paige turns to Rhiannon with a smile. "And now, back to why we're here today. Please, can we continue the tour of your delightful studio? I believe you've got some models coming in to show off some of your designs?"

"That's right." Rhiannon nods. "On with the show!"

Mom and I exchange glances as we leave Eliza's office. I think we're both proud—and more than a little impressed—with how Paige handled that, at the end, at least. I am curious as to whether or not any of that footage will actually make the show. But like Paige said, our fans probably have a right to hear the truth. So often the tabloid rags bury it. It's refreshing when it's allowed to surface and shine, kind of like taking a shower after a mud bath.

Chapter
10

After the success of our short New York trip, Paige and I both agree that Mom should come with us to Milan Fashion Week in September. I'm hoping that if Fran's recovery continues as well as it's been going, she might be able to come too—not with the heavy load of all her old responsibilities, but in a partnership with Mom. I think all of us would benefit from this combination. I plan to pitch the idea to Helen as soon as we meet again after our short hiatus.

It's interesting that while our show's cast and crew are on vacation, Blake and Ben's new show has just gone into production. That's because their network was so enthused over the idea that they wanted to launch it as soon as possible. Already there's a good buzz going on about the new reality show.

"August would be the perfect time for you and Paige to make an appearance on our show," Blake tells me as we're on our way home following a movie premiere that Ben got him tickets to. The sci-fi movie was kind of ho-hum, but I have to admit it was fun being involved in the splashy premiere. Fortunately Paige played my fashion consultant, dressing me in a sophisticated Badgley Mischka cocktail dress in a cool shade of pewter. And it was amusing that cameras were flashing at Blake and me as we made our exit out of the theater.

Seriously, just one year ago I never could've imagined that I'd be involved in this kind of lifestyle. Although I disliked it at first, I guess it's kind of grown on me, probably because I have a strong suspicion it will only be one short era of my life. It's kind of like a rollercoaster ride—it's fun while it lasts, but it'll be good to get off.

"And just what would Paige and I do if we did make an appearance?" I ask Blake. "Would you send Paige, an engaged young woman whose relationship has been a bit bumpy already, on a blind date?"

"No, of course not. Like Ben suggested, Paige could do some fashion advising. It would be a great way to cross-promote your show."

"Our show's on hiatus."

"Yes, but publicity is publicity."

"So I've heard."

"And *you're* not engaged," he points out.

Now for some reason the way he says this aggravates me. As if he's not involved with me at all—like we're nothing more than just friends. I honestly thought we were more than that. "That's right," I retort. "I'm not engaged. So do you want to send me on a blind date?"

He chuckles. "It might be interesting."

"And who, might I ask, would choose this date for me?"

"The computer dating service. You'd fill out the questionnaire and they would try to find a match."

"Have you done that?" I ask him.

"Sure, Ben and I both did it a couple weeks ago. How else could we go on blind dates?"

"Right ..." Not for the first time, I'm questioning the sensibility of this whole thing. Is it right to go on a blind date for the sake of a TV show? On the one hand, like Blake says, it could be educational for viewers. On the other hand, what if hearts get broken? Like mine. "So have you gone on a blind date for the show yet?"

He lets out a long sigh. "Actually, I had a coffee date just last week."

"Really?" I'm surprised. "You never told me."

"Hey, it's work. You don't always tell me about your work."

"I don't date anyone at work."

He glances at me. "Are you saying you're jealous?"

Suddenly I feel set up, or cornered, or something. I just shrug. "Not exactly. I guess I'm more curious. Was your date a match from the computer?"

"Kind of. We started out with a small pool of daters ... you know, for the sake of the show."

"Like people from *Malibu Beach* and friends of Ben?"

"Yeah. The dating service matched us up from that pool and that's how the show begins."

"Do the viewers know this?" I ask. "Or do they think you went out with a girl who was pulled out of a million potential dates?"

"We don't mention the small pool, but I think viewers will figure it out when they see the same people going on other dates ... but the pool will get bigger and bigger."

"Kind of a pyramid pool?" I tease.

"We have to keep it interesting."

"Yeah, I can imagine. So is it going to end up being like *The Bachelor*?"

"What do you mean?"

"You know, people drinking too much, making out, going to bed?"

"No—at least I don't think so. Not with me anyway."

"But with others?"

He shrugs. "That's not the focus of the show, but I suppose it could happen."

Now, call me old-fashioned (and plenty of people do), but that just aggravates me. I don't like it that Blake is involved in something like this.

"So, are you saying you wouldn't go on a blind date?" he persists. "Just for the fun of it?"

"Why would I want to do that?"

"Because it would be interesting, Erin. Wouldn't you like to see what kind of guy the computer matches you with?"

"Out of your *small* pool?" I frown. "What if I ended up with Ben? Ugh!"

"Ben's not the devil, Erin."

"I know. But I couldn't stand to be stuck on a blind date with him. What would happen if I agreed to do this and hated the guy and walked out?"

"That would be your choice. No way are we forcing anyone to do anything. That's what makes it interesting."

"Right …"

"What if you agreed to a blind date and the computer matched you with me?" he asks in a hopeful tone.

I laugh. "That wouldn't exactly be a blind date … or anything that your viewers would be interested in."

"Maybe not."

Suddenly I feel like calling his bluff. Not that it's a bluff exactly. But since he's jabbed me in a jealous spot, I decide to jab him back. "You know, Blake, it might be interesting after all."

"Really?"

"Yeah. I do wonder what kind of guy the computer would match me with. I mean, I'd be totally honest in my likes and dislikes. Maybe I'd meet a really cool guy."

"Maybe . . ." He sounds uncertain.

"I would only agree to do it if you let me be part of the big pool of daters. Not just the handpicked ones."

"I guess we could arrange that."

"Okay. If you do that, I'll give it a try."

"I'll talk to Ben." Blake sounds a little doubtful, and I suppose I feel a bit smug, like I have him over the old proverbial barrel. I like that.

Although I follow Blake's direction by registering with the on-line dating service the following week, I go for almost two weeks without hearing a word. Really, I'm relieved. By late August I'm thinking I was nuts to even agree to anything so ridiculous. But Paige and I did accept the invitation to guest star a couple of times in order to offer fashion critique and suggestions.

Actually, I played my old role as "Camera Girl" so we could get some footage for our show. Meanwhile, Paige handled the actual consultations with the girls who were getting ready for their big blind dates. I'll admit it was kind of fun, but I know I wouldn't want to be in their shoes—it's obviously nerve-wracking. Not only are they putting themselves out there with guys they've never met, they're doing it in front of the whole world. Not my cup of tea.

So when the producer of their show calls me after Labor Day to say that the online service has matched me with someone, I'm quite naturally hesitant.

"Oh, I don't know," I tell him. "I think maybe I've changed my mind."

"But wait until you hear more," he says eagerly. "We decided to play up the angle that you and Blake are involved with each other. I know you're not in an exclusive relationship or anything like that. Still, you have dated. So what we want to do is send the two of you on a *double* blind date!"

"A double blind date?"

"Yes. We've found great matches for both you and Blake and we want to send the four of you out on what we call an über-date."

"An über-date?"

"Usually, our dates are budget dates. Sometimes just coffee, sometimes lunch. But an über-date is when we pull out all the stops and send you to some new hotspot for a fantastic evening. Surely, you can't say no to that, Erin?"

"And Blake thought this would be a good idea? A double blind date with him and me?"

"Absolutely."

Okay, while I'm somewhat irritated, I'm also intrigued. The producer continues to pitch this double blind date as the greatest thing short of winning the lottery. Finally, my curiosity gets the best of me and I agree. He fills me in on the details and the big date is set for Saturday, only four days from now. But as soon as I hang up I'm questioning myself. Have I completely lost my mind?

Naturally, Paige thinks this is hilarious. "I'll bet Blake set himself up with a total babe, Erin. And you'll be stuck with a loser."

"Blake assured me he has no control over the selection of the dates," I tell her.

"And you believed him? Erin, this is *reality* TV. Get real."

"Well, I've already considered that possibility," I admit. "And even if I'm paired with the nerdiest guy imaginable, I'll treat him politely."

"Good for you. It's always best to take the high road." She grins. "And just in case you get punked with your date, you need to look absolutely stunning. So you'll let me help, won't you?"

I shrug. "Why not?"

"We should make a deal with *Celebrity Blind Date* to use some of the footage of your date in our show."

"I don't know about that. If I end up looking stupid on their show, I'm not sure I want to do it again on ours."

"Well, we won't use the footage if it's really horrible, Erin. But just in case, let me ask Mom to help with the legal end. That way we can use anything we want from our show's wardrobe for your date. And Leah said that some new things have arrived for Milan already." Paige rubs her hands together. "I can't wait to check it out."

So Paige and I spend Friday afternoon "shopping" in our own wardrobe department until she finally settles on what she says is a killer outfit. I'll admit it's hot. "Although I'm not sure about these shoes," I tell her. "The heels are a little high for me."

"But they're Prada and they make your legs look long. Plus they're beyond perfect with the Miu Miu dress. Besides, you said this is a fancy date. So I'm guessing you'll be dining someplace really swanky. You need to look great, Erin. Not just for the sake of our show, but so that Blake can't keep his eyes off you."

"Don't you mean *my* date won't be able to?"

"I mean *both* of them, Erin."

I laugh but give in to my sister's fashion sensibility. I might not admit it, but she's right. I do want to capture Blake's attention.

On Saturday, about thirty minutes before my "date" is supposed to pick me up, a *Celebrity Blind Date* camera guy arrives. To my surprise he's accompanied by the show's host, none other than Benjamin Kross. Fortunately, Paige takes it all in stride, breaking the ice with some jokes. Then the focus turns to me.

"We're at the home of Erin Forrester," Ben says to the camera, "where she's been getting ready for her big blind date tonight." He smiles at me. "You look fantastic, Erin. Let me guess ... did your fashionista sister have anything to do with your look?"

I tell him a bit about what I'm wearing. "Paige and I are getting ready to head to Italy for Milan Fashion Week," I say as a plug for our show. "*On the Runway* will be shooting on location there in a couple of weeks. That's why I'm wearing Italian designers tonight."

"Well, you look stunning. Your date is one lucky guy. But what about poor Blake? We know that you and he have dated off and on over the past few years. Do you think he'll be so distracted by your loveliness that he'll forget about his own date?"

I laugh. "I doubt it. And even if he were distracted, Blake is a gentleman."

"Yes, I have to agree with you there. So, Erin, tell us a bit about yourself and how you filled out the application with the online dating service."

I pause to think. "Well, I mentioned my interest in the film industry and how I love photography and the arts."

"What is your favorite thing to photograph?"

"Anything in nature," I say quickly. "I also like architecture."

"And your ideal date would be?"

I press my lips together. "Probably doing something outdoors. Maybe a hike ... taking some photos ... then going to a quaint restaurant and eating outdoors."

He nods, glancing at my feet. "You're certainly not wearing your hiking shoes tonight."

I force a smile. "Paige urged me to wear these shoes."

"Only because they look absolutely fabulous on you," she says. Just then our bell rings, and the camera guy follows me as I answer it.

A tall, good-looking guy (not a geek) is holding out a small bouquet of daisies. "Hi, I'm Aidan," he tells me with a great smile. His sparkling blue eyes seem to contrast with his curly dark brown hair. All in all, this guy is well put together. No one is punking me.

"I'm Erin," I tell him. "Thanks." I take the flowers and wonder what to do with them. "I love daisies!" I see Paige smiling from the shadows as she gives me a quick thumbs-up.

"I hoped you would." He looks a little uneasy.

"This is kind of weird, isn't it?" I say. "The whole blind date thing?"

He nods. "I was questioning it myself on the way over here."

"Let me put these in some water," I say, but as I turn around, Paige swoops them from me. When she returns from the kitchen, I introduce her to Aiden. "You may have seen Paige on our TV show."

He blinks. "You have a TV show?"

Paige giggles. "Obviously, you haven't seen it." Then she quickly explains.

"Paige is the queen of style," Ben tells Aidan. "She broke all the single guys' hearts when she got engaged a few months ago."

"Poor Ben," she says mockingly.

"And now, boys and girls"—Ben claps his hands—"we need to rock and roll. Our limo awaits."

Feeling understandably nervous, Aidan and I go down to the limo with cameras rolling. He politely opens the door for me and there, already in the limo, are Blake and a strikingly pretty brunette.

"This is Grace," Blake tells us as Aidan and I slide into the seat across from them. One camera guy and Ben sit in the back. Soon we are introduced all around and although we make some small talk, I'm distracted by the fact that Blake and Grace are in casual clothes. That's when I notice that Aidan is relatively casual-looking too. Suddenly I feel overdressed and don't know what to do. The limo is on its way and it's too late to ask to go back to change.

"No one told me exactly where we're going tonight," I say to Ben. "Somehow I got the impression it was a dressy affair. Seems I was wrong."

"Didn't Blake tell you?" Ben glances over at Blake, who looks blank.

"I'm sorry," Blake says. "I thought Ben told you."

"We're going sailing on this amazing boat," Ben explains. "Catalina Island and a fantastic catered dinner."

"Right ..." I look down at my high heels and frown. "I wish I'd known."

Before long we're aboard a very cool boat—a boat I could've really enjoyed had I known we were going sailing. And after a short tour where Grace and the guys actually do some hands-on with the sails and such, we are served a casual-but-nice dinner out on the aft deck. And I know it should be no big deal, but it's like I got off on the wrong foot—literally. As the evening progresses, despite taking off my shoes, I continue to feel out of step.

Meanwhile, Grace is relaxed and lovely and charming—and I begin to realize that she is capturing the attention of both guys. She's a Dodgers fan and talks about baseball like an expert. She's also naturally gregarious, but not in an obnoxious way. She's great at drawing out interesting conversation, though it's hard for me to get a word in edgewise. Maybe I'm not trying hard enough, or perhaps I'm just mesmerized. Like, where did this girl come from? So I ask her.

"I grew up on a little ranch not far from Santa Barbara," she tells me. "My dad always dreamed of being a cowboy."

"So do you have horses?" Blake asks.

"Oh, yeah." She nods. "About a dozen. And some cattle too, as well as some other animals."

"Do you ride?" Aidan asks.

"Sure. My brother and I grew up riding."

Now both guys pepper Grace with questions about the ranch and horses and her brother, who used to do professional rodeo. I just listen—it's as if I'm not even here. I'm fully aware that the cameras are running and I'm going to end up looking like the dummy date. It's like I just can't get into sync. In fact, I'm pretty sure no one would notice if I disappeared.

So I excuse myself before dessert and slip away to the other end of the boat. I briefly consider jumping ship and swimming to shore, but the lights of Catalina look to be at least a mile away. Instead, I decide to just sit here for a bit, soaking in the starlit sky, enjoying the lapping sound of water and the peace.

"Hey, what are you doing over here?" Blake asks me.

"Just enjoying the view." I stand up. "Sorry. I guess I lost track of the time."

"At least you didn't fall overboard. Are you going to rejoin the group?"

"Sure." I start walking back.

"Are you okay, Erin?"

"Yeah." I nod. "I just feel a little out of it."

"That Grace is quite a talker."

"But a pleasant talker."

"Aidan seems to like her too."

I laugh. "So, really, I wouldn't be missed if I just continued to lay low."

"There you are," says Ben as he comes for us with a camera guy. "Everything okay?"

"Everything's great," I tell him. "I just got caught up in the view. It's spectacular back there without all the boat lights."

"Well, they just brought in dessert," Ben tells me with a trace of irritation in his voice. "Hopefully you'll want to participate now."

Soon we're all seated at the table again. As the dessert tray is served, Ben moves into his role as the host, asking us about our date experience, what we liked, what we didn't like. Everyone seems happy and pleased, except for me.

"I guess I'm just not the blind dating type," I admit. "I

don't really like surprises that much. And I wish I'd known more about our date destination earlier."

"You felt overdressed?" Ben asks.

"Yes. And I might've brought my camera along. I mean, this boat trip has been beautiful. No complaints there."

"Aren't you happy with your date?" he persists. "Something wrong with Aidan here?" He grins at Aidan. "Seems like a nice enough fellow to me."

"Aidan is great," I admit. "But the whole thing ... well, it just feels a little awkward. To me, anyway. I'm sure most people would love doing something like this. Maybe I'm just weird." I actually look to Blake, wishing he would do or say something to help bail me out of this. It's like I keep digging myself deeper into a hole.

"It's probably my fault," Grace says. "I talk too much when I'm nervous."

"You don't seem nervous," Ben tells her.

"Oh, I'm just good at covering it up," she says. "I'm pretty nervous. I mean, most of you have TV experience, and I'm just a regular girl."

"You don't seem like a regular girl to me," Blake says with real admiration.

"I thought you were totally comfortable," Aidan adds.

"I'm even thinking about inviting you to join our regular cast of daters," Ben tells her. "You've been great. Now, tell me, Grace, what did you especially like about Blake?"

She looks at Blake then slowly smiles. "He's a real gentleman. He's a good listener, but he's also a great conversationalist. He's funny and fun."

"So, would you go out with him again?" Ben asks.

"Absolutely." She nods.

"How about you, Blake? Would you do a second date?"

Blake looks uncomfortable and I suspect it's because of me.

"Sure, he would," I answer for him. "Wouldn't you, Blake?"

He just shrugs.

"And how would you feel about that, Erin?" Ben asks. "I know you and Blake have dated some."

"I think Grace is a very nice person." I smile at her. "Anyone would be fortunate to go out with her."

"Well, thank you," she tells me.

"So ... Aidan?" Ben turns to him now. "Would you want a second date with Erin?"

Aidan looks like he's at a loss for words. So once again, I step in. "I'm sure Aidan would prefer going out with someone more like Grace," I tell him. "I have to admit I've been kind of a stick-in-the-mud tonight." I smile at Aidan. "My apologies. I probably shouldn't have agreed to do this. Like I said, I'm just not the blind date type."

They continue to chat some more and I feel like actually jumping overboard now. I can't even explain what's going on with me. Maybe it's PMS or something, but I feel like I'm on the edge of tears, and the sooner this night ends, the happier I will be. Is it because Aidan seems uninterested, or that I'm jealous of Grace, or simply that I feel hurt by Blake? Maybe it's all three; I don't know. But I do know one thing: I won't be watching this particular episode of *Celebrity Blind Date*.

Chapter
11

Blake is somewhat apologetic the following week. We go out for our usual date on Friday and have a pretty good time, but I feel off balance and confused. I'm just not too sure about our relationship anymore. I know it's because I had assumed things were going to change between us, in a good way, and then they didn't. Also there's that whole blind date thing ... and Grace, who, to my surprise, has become a regular part of the dating cast. I can tell that Blake still thinks she's pretty cool. Is there more to it than that? I don't know. I feel worried. And Blake is so caught up in the TV show that he seems oblivious.

As a result, I'm very glad to go back to work on our show, and planning for the Milan trip is a good distraction. This time I decide to follow Paige's example and do my research. Mollie becomes my study buddy, a plan that has a twofold reasoning on my part. Obviously, I really need someone to help me brush up on Italian fashion so I can hold my own against Paige. But the larger reason is I know Mollie's a little bummed that she's not back in school yet. "Winter term will be here soon enough," I reassure her. And I tell her that she's wise to give herself—and Fern—more time to adjust. Fortunately, she seems to have moved well beyond the baby blues or post-partum depression or whatever it was, and most of the time she seems pretty normal. And she's more than happy to help me. This research is a natural fit for Mollie—she loves following fashion and the names of the designers roll off her tongue almost as easily as they do for Paige.

"It's a good thing the show isn't dependent on you for your fashion expertise," Mollie tells me two days before we're scheduled to leave for Italy. She's been quizzing me on designers all evening.

"Hey, I mistook Rossi for Rosso—so sue me."

"Well, Sergio Rossi might sue you if he heard you saying that Renzo Rosso launched the Eco Pump." Mollie shakes her head like she can't believe how dense I am. "And Rosso might sue you if you said that Rossi owned Diesel."

"Maybe I should just forget about both of them—if I can't keep them straight, what's the point?"

"The reason I told you about Sergio *Rossi*," she persists, "is because I thought you'd appreciate his commitment to sustainability. The Eco Pump is a *biodegradable* shoe, Erin. He uses this stuff called Liquid Wood for the heel and the sole. Plus he treats the leather with an ecological tanning process. And part of the profits from his sales go to Good Planet. I thought you'd like to mention that, if you get the chance."

"Right." I nod. "I remember now."

"And Renzo *Rosso* is of interest because of Diesel. You said you like Diesel designs."

"You're right. I do. But right now my head is so full of names like Pucci and Prada and Versace and Gucci and Biagiotti and Balestra. It's like I'm suddenly hungry for linguini."

"Oh, don't rub it in." She groans. "Thinking about the food you guys will have in Italy is torturous. I only read the first half of *Eat, Pray, Love* while I was pregnant, but I was craving Italian food for weeks after that. No wonder I piled on the pounds before Fern was born."

"So there's a reason to be thankful you don't have to go to Milan," I tell her.

She rolls her eyes. "Will you be worried about Blake while you're gone?"

"Why should I be?"

"Well, it sounded like he was kind of into that Grace chick."

"I never said that," I argue. Which is true; I didn't tell her that. In fact, I said very little about the whole blind date thing. It's something I want to forget. "What makes you think Blake's into Grace?"

Mollie looks uneasy. "I guess it was something Tony said."

"What?" I demand.

"Just that Blake thinks Grace is pretty cool."

I nod. "She *is* pretty cool. I like her too."

"And you're okay that Blake's spending time with her?"

I'm not sure what to say.

"I mean on the show. Tony said she's already become part of the regular cast."

"Tony sure seems to know a lot about it." I'm gathering up my stuff, thinking I should get home since tomorrow's my last day to get organized before we leave for Italy. "Has he been spending a lot of time with Blake?"

"I think he's trying to get some hands-on experience with the show."

"Is he going to do a blind date?"

"Sounds like it."

"And you're okay with that?"

She holds up her hands. "Like I told you, Erin. Tony and I are just hanging together as friends these days. Kind of like you and Blake."

"Right . . ."

Mollie narrows her eyes. "And you're okay with that, aren't you?"

"What?"

"You and Blake just being friends?"

I shrug. "I guess so."

Mollie gets a knowing look. "You're not."

"I don't know," I admit.

"Well, I think you're jealous of Grace," she says a bit smugly.

I roll my eyes. "Maybe I am. Or maybe I'm not. I don't even know. But I do know I need to go. I don't have time to think about this now."

"And if, while you're gone, Blake and Grace start to date . . . you're okay with that?"

"If that's what they want, sure. Why not?"

Mollie looks doubtful, but to my relief doesn't say anything.

"Look, if Blake and I are meant to be together, it'll happen, right?"

She nods. "Right. It'll happen."

"Tomorrow's a crazy day for me," I tell her. "We have planning meetings and I still need to pack. So I might not see you again before we leave." I hug her.

"Drop me a text or two if you're not too busy," she tells me. "I'll be praying for your trip."

"Thanks." It's a relief to see Mollie's faith is still intact—perhaps even stronger than before. I lean down and kiss baby Fern good-bye. "Now don't you grow up while I'm gone."

As I drive home I try not to obsess over what Mollie insinuated about Blake and Grace. Really, I have no control over what does or doesn't happen between them. At least Blake and I are good friends now. Although we haven't spent as much time together since *Celebrity Blind Date* went into production, I know that our friendship is the most solid it's been for a while—and way better than when I went to the Bahamas and figured we were finished. And I value our friendship. Even if that's all it's meant to be, I should be thankful.

The doctor decided, and Fran reluctantly agreed, that it's too soon for her to travel abroad. Although she's feeling much better and is able to care for herself, an overseas trip is just not in the cards right now. Her mom was hugely relieved to see Fran's improvement and went home to Boston last week—and I'm sure Fran was hugely relieved to see her go. Even though Fran can't go to Milan, I think it's been good medicine for her to participate in the plans for this trip. And she'll continue to play a consultant role from her home. Plus she assured us that she intends to be well enough to come on the next trip we take.

After the stresses of the Bahamas trip, Mom had really hoped that Fran would be up for this one, and Helen had planned for them to direct in tandem, lightening the load. At least Leah gets to come now. Naturally, Leah is thrilled, but Paige is concerned. For some reason Paige doesn't completely trust Leah's ability to direct or produce. Paige only sees her as a motivated assistant—not someone with producer abilities. I'm not sure. I guess we'll have to see.

"I have something special planned for this trip," Leah tells us as we're boarding the flight to Milan. She points to me. "Which is why I asked you to bring your camcorder. My carry-on bag is full of accessories and beauty items I gathered from a couple of sponsors last week. We're going to give some lucky passengers in-flight makeovers."

"Seriously?" I glance around the first-class section, wondering how these people will react to a fashion intervention.

"We might have to start in the coach section," Mom suggests.

"What about the flight attendants?" Paige looks worried. "Will they think we're a security risk?"

"We've already gotten permission from the airline," Mom explains. Obviously she and Leah have been in cahoots. "The airline appreciates the free publicity we'll be giving them."

"If all goes well, they might even buy some ad time on the show," Leah says.

Paige smiles. "Well, this could be fun." She points at me. "Let's start with you."

"Right," I say sarcastically. "I'll film myself while you make me over."

"We'll do you off camera," Paige says. "That way the passengers will see two good examples of travel chic."

"Travel chic?"

She nods as she reaches for her own carry-on. "That's what I'm going to call this." And just like that, she's working me over. "At least you're wearing a cool set of sweats," she tells me. "But you need some color and sparkle." I let her do her thing as a middle-aged woman across the aisle watches with interest.

"You're very good at that," she tells Paige. Paige explains who we are and why we're doing this and asks the woman if she'd like a minimakeover too. At first the woman is hesitant.

"Oh, come on, Mona," the guy with her urges. "What can it hurt? And it'll pass the time."

So Leah gets Mona to sign a release paper, and with my camera running, Paige begins her magic. Because my sister is so cheerful and upbeat, Mona actually begins to relax and has a good time as Paige perks up her makeup, helps her with her hair, adds a scarf, and tries out some accessories.

"And I get to keep these?" Mona asks as she puts on a pair of silver earrings.

"All the accessories are compliments of Banana Republic and Bluefly dot-com," Leah explains.

"You look great," the guy tells Mona when Paige has finished her magic.

Leah pulls out a hand mirror and gives it to Mona.

"See," Paige says with satisfaction. *"Travel chic."*

When our flight is somewhere over the Atlantic and food-and-beverage service is taking a break, we emerge from the first-class section to seek more takers. I continue to film Paige as she approaches her first "lucky" coach-class candidate—a young woman dressed in frumpy sweats, with her hair pulled back in a stark ponytail.

"Hi," Paige says cheerfully. "I'm Paige Forrester from *On the Runway* and I'd like to give you a minimakeover."

The woman blinks. *"What?"*

"We're on our way to Fashion Week in Milan," Paige explains. "And we thought it would be fun to help some passengers arrive at their destination looking travel chic."

"Travel chic?"

"I know how lots of travelers just crawl out of bed, don't take any time with their appearance, and arrive looking like something the cat dragged in."

The woman laughs. "That's true." She agrees to participate, and after about twenty minutes, Paige has this woman looking great too.

Paige does about a dozen travel chic makeovers. Some women only need a light touch, accessories, and some lip gloss. Some need major help. Finally, despite the increased interest in being made over, Paige and I are both ready for a break. Before we return to first class, we get a solid round of applause from the pleased passengers.

"That went well," I tell Leah and Mom as we return to our seats.

"Yeah." Paige nods. "Fun idea."

"Now you girls might want to get some rest," Mom advises. "We have a busy schedule in Milan."

With a connection in Zurich and eighteen hours of travel time, we're all fairly exhausted when we land, but on the way to the hotel, I feel energized by the beauty of Milan. "I can't wait to get out there with my camera," I tell Mom.

"Well, it's your free day to do as you like," Leah says. "Make the most of it, because tomorrow, we shift into full speed."

"We're staying in a former convent," Mom informs us.

"Are you kidding?" Paige asks.

She laughs. "Not at all. It's a smallish Four Seasons hotel near the Via della Spiga and it's supposed to be quite nice."

As it turns out, the hotel is very nice, with a great Italian feel to it. Paige and I share the suite this time, and Mom and Leah share an adjoining room.

"I know Dylan's going to be in Milan," I say to Paige as we're getting situated in our room. "I hope you'll respect me enough not to invite him for a sleepover here."

She rolls her eyes. "Taking that whole convent thing a bit seriously, are we?"

"You know how I feel about it — engaged or not engaged, I think you should wait until after the wedding."

"I know." She sighs. "My old-fashioned little sister."

"Maybe so. But considering how things went — or nearly went — in the Bahamas, I'd think you might want to reconsider the whole sleeping together thing even more now."

"Why?" Paige asks as she starts unpacking her carry-on.

"Well, if Dylan had really had an affair with Eliza, would you have broken off your engagement?"

"Maybe ..." She sets her cosmetics bag on the bathroom's travertine countertop.

"And would you have regretted having had sex with him?"

"Maybe ..." She turns and looks at me. "So that's why you think it's wrong to have sex? Because we might not get married in the end?"

"I saw how hurt you were after the Bahamas, Paige. And I could be wrong, but I think a big part of that hurt was the result of having been so intimate with Dylan. It's like you gave your heart and everything to him. You totally trusted him with all of you — and then it seemed like he just stomped on it. I mean, he didn't really, because he didn't really cheat on you. At least we don't think he did."

"But if he *had* actually cheated, you think it would hurt me even more because I'd had sex with him?"

"You're the only one who can answer that for sure, Paige. Honestly, if it were me — if I trusted someone like that and then he betrayed me? Really, it would hurt a lot!"

She seems to be considering this. "You know, you could be right."

"And maybe if you weren't having sex with him ... well, maybe it would be better for both of you, and for your relationship in general."

She shrugs. "I don't know ... but I guess I'll think about it."

The rest of our bags are delivered and we continue to unpack. I'm thinking perhaps, just perhaps, I made a little progress with Paige. I really think she's more vulnerable than she realizes when it comes to her relationship with Dylan. And sometimes I wonder if the engagement might not have simply been a handy escape for both of them. I remember how freaked Paige had been in London, thanks to the media frenzy over her alleged relationship with Benjamin Kross. The paparazzi got the best of her and she even considered stepping out of the spotlight permanently.

And then, like a knight on a white horse, Dylan showed up and rescued her with an engagement ring. But we later learned that his design firm was having a serious struggle. His reception in Paris had gone from poor to positive due to my sister, but the critics had turned on him shortly after his show, and getting engaged to a fashionista like Paige gave him a nice PR boost. So what if both of their motives were more about convenience than love?

Chapter
12

Milan is amazing! The architecture, the gardens, the river, the light—it's all a photographer's paradise. But by the end of my "free" day I am so tired I feel like I can barely focus my eyes, let alone my camera lens. By the time I drag myself back to the hotel, I'm so exhausted that I can't even remember my room number. I actually call my mom from the elevator, waking her up to find out which floor to get out on.

"I'm glad you're back," she tells me. "At least I can sleep more soundly now."

When I get to our suite, to my surprise Paige is already there, and looks as beat as I am. She's already in her pajamas, with a partially-eaten room-service meal in front of her. "I know it's early," she tells me. "But I plan to crash any minute now." She points to the food. "And I ordered way too much, so if you're interested, have at it."

I take her up on the offer. As she heads for bed, I polish off her leftover dinner of pasta and shrimp, which is delicious. Then I take a shower and am in bed at just a little past seven — and Paige is already fast asleep.

I wake up early the next morning, pull on some sweats, and head downstairs to get some espresso. Sitting outside at the veranda restaurant, enjoying the beautiful morning light, I decide that I totally love Milan. I check my phone and am surprised to hear a voicemail from Blake.

"Hey, Erin," he says. "Sorry I missed seeing you off yesterday. I really meant to make it over to tell you good-bye. I hope you're having a great time in Milan. I can't help but feel envious. Maybe I'll see if we can arrange some international blind dates." He laughs. "Have fun!"

Since I think it must be late at night there now, I send him a text, telling him that we're here and that I love Milan. I try to think of something more to say, but suddenly I'm replaying Mollie's words about Blake and Grace. How would I feel if they started to date? The thought of that just shuts me down, so I hit send and put my iPhone back in my bag. I check out the menu and have just placed my order when I see my mom coming out to the veranda.

"There you are," she says as she comes over to my table. "I was hoping you were down here." She sits across from me. "Isn't this absolutely lovely?"

I nod. "Great hotel, Mom."

She smiles. "I could get used to this."

"So, what's on the docket this morning?" I ask as she peruses the menu.

"Well, you've heard of that new Italian designer, Alberto Baggatio, haven't you?"

I try to remember then nod. "Yes. He used to be with Gucci, right?"

"Yes. That's right." She pauses to place her breakfast order and I'm impressed that her Italian is not too bad. "So anyway, we've got an interview appointment with him at his studio. His show is Saturday, so he's busy, but his people seemed happy to squeeze us in at eleven o'clock. As a result we'll have to keep it short. I promised them it would take less than an hour."

I glance at my watch, surprised to see it's only seven thirty.

"Shawna and Luis should be at the hotel by nine," she tells me. "And we'll leave here around ten thirty. The Baggatio studio is only about fifteen minutes from here."

"Sounds good."

"I made sure Paige was up. I know how much time she needs to get ready."

"Great."

I tell Mom about the conversation I had with Paige yesterday and my concerns about her and Dylan. "I wasn't trying to be preachy," I explain, "but I am worried that she's opening herself up to be hurt again."

Mom frowns. "Do you have any real reason to think that Dylan isn't sincere about their engagement?"

I tell her a bit about the critical fallout after the Paris show and how Dylan's design career seems to be failing. "You have to admit that it was convenient publicity for him to link himself to Paige."

"Yes . . . but he seemed so sincere in New York. I hoped all that would be behind us now."

"Maybe it is." We pause our conversation as our food is served. I almost wish I hadn't mentioned anything about Paige and Dylan at all. Really, why should I care so much? They have to live their own lives.

"I wish Jon could see this place," Mom says wistfully.

"It's really romantic, isn't it?"

She smiles as she reaches for her espresso. "Very."

"I was just texting Blake about it. I told him I think I'm in love with Milan."

"Speaking of Blake . . ." She looks curiously at me. "I can never figure you two out. Are you still seriously dating him or not? I know that whole *Celebrity Blind Date* show kind of shook you up."

"They could've called it *Blindsided* as far as I was concerned," I admit.

She shakes her head. "It seemed an odd idea to me — sending you and him on a double date, but not as a couple."

"And that other girl — her name's Grace — she pretty much dominated the whole evening. Not in a bad way either. In fact, she reminded me a little of Paige — you know, with that gift of charm and beauty that I don't have."

"Sounds frustrating."

"It was. Before I left for this trip Mollie asked me how I'd feel if Blake started to date Grace. I mean, outside the show."

"How would you feel?"

I'm surprised that I've opened up this much with Mom. But since I've already gotten this far, I decide it probably doesn't matter. "Well, I was just thinking about it. I think I would feel a little bit sad."

"For so long you've said that you and Blake were only good friends, Erin. Have you really changed your opinion on that? Or do you think it's a case of wanting something that someone else wants?"

"To be honest, I'm not sure. Even before Grace came along, I was starting to think I might be ready for a more serious relationship with Blake. I mean, he's asked about being exclusive before, but I always kind of blew him off." Then I confess to her how I'd hoped that he was going to bring it up again awhile back. "He'd called to say he had something important to talk about."

"And you thought he was going to ask about being exclusive?"

I nod. "It was silly, I know. Especially considering how I've acted. When I realized he only wanted to talk about the new reality show, I was kind of hurt."

Mom laughs, but not in a mean way. "I'm sorry, Erin."

I force a smile. "I'm sure I deserved it."

"So ... if he'd asked, what would you have said?"

"Honestly?" I consider this. "I think I might've said yes. That's why it hurt so much."

She pats my hand. "You know, I'm glad to hear that, Erin."

I blink. "Huh?"

"Not the part about you getting hurt. The part about you being willing to commit."

"Why?"

"Oh, I've wondered if you were going to have some commitment issues."

"Commitment issues?" Although I feign surprise, this is something I've actually wondered about myself.

"Well, I know that losing your dad was hard on you." She sighs. "It was hard on all of us. Then you and Blake were so serious throughout high school, and when he broke your heart ... well, I worried that you were kind of pushing other guys away too. Like Lionel. He seemed to really like you. And Paige told me about the young man in Paris—the one from Hermès?"

I smile. "Gabin."

"Yes. Paige thought you really liked him and she said she thought he was smitten with you. But you pushed him away too."

"That was because Blake showed up," I admit.

"Aha." Mom grins. "So perhaps you like Blake more than you realized."

"Maybe." I shrug, trying to figure this out, and wondering why it's so hard. "But Gabin's awfully nice too."

"Will he be here this week?"

"Good question. I wouldn't be surprised."

"We're scheduled for the Hermès show," Mom tells me as she checks her notebook. "In fact, it's tomorrow afternoon."

"Well, maybe you'll get to meet Gabin then."

"I hope so."

We finish our breakfast and run into Luis and Shawna on our way to the elevator. "Nice digs," Shawna says as we ride up.

"How's your place?" I ask as we walk through the elegant lobby.

"Not bad." She wrinkles her nose. "But not as posh as this."

Soon Paige and I are being coiffed and made up, and Leah and Mom are going over today's schedule.

"Why is the visit to Gucci scheduled so late in the day?" Paige asks.

"They wanted to do it after hours," Leah explains.

Paige makes a disappointed face. "But I made dinner plans with Dylan."

"Then you'll have to change them," Mom tells her. "Your first priority here is the show, Paige."

"I know."

"When did Dylan arrive?" I ask as Luis gives me a quick mist of hairspray and then fluffs my hair.

"He gets here this afternoon."

"We have you girls scheduled to attend his show on Friday," Leah points out.

"And there's the Louis Vuitton after-party tonight," Mom reminds us. "I'm sure you can spend time with Dylan there."

"What time is the Louis Vuitton show?" Paige asks.

"Right after the Ricci show," Mom tells her. "It'll be a busy afternoon."

"It'll be a busy week," Leah clarifies.

The Baggatio studio is surprisingly calm considering that their show is just days away. We do the usual studio tour, and then we're introduced to Alberto Baggatio. He greets both of us then turns to Paige with a big smile. "I am so pleased to meet you, Miss Forrester," he says as he takes her hand.

"Please, call me Paige."

"Then you must call me Alberto," he says as the three of us sit down in the leather chairs in his office. "I am so impressed with your fashion sense. I have seen your show and you are wise beyond your years. I would be pleased to have someone with such a fine-tuned sense of style in my studio."

"Thank you." She crosses her legs then leans forward. "And I am a great admirer of yours, Alberto. I've been following your career for some time now."

"Then I must ask. Did you come to my show in Paris?"

She nods. "I did. And not only did I love your line, but I was very impressed with your selection of models."

He chuckles. "There was a mixed reaction to that."

Paige turns to me now. "Alberto featured models that look like real women," she explains. "Including Laetitia Casta, Bar

Rafaeli, and Adriana Lima. Beautiful women, but not your typical runway models. And I believe you had Elle Macpherson as well."

"Some say I copied Marc Jacobs," he admits. "I say imitation is the highest form of flattery."

"I agree."

"Marc started something admirable. I am only trying to continue the tradition."

"Will you continue it in Milan?"

He nods. "I love using models who look like real women. I love curves on a woman's body. It's what I design for."

Okay, I'm really impressed now. "I think that's wonderful," I tell him. "I get concerned when so many of the fashion images we see are stick-thin models. That's not at all what most women look like."

"I am in agreement. Oh, I understand how tall, thin models make some clothes look good. But I say if you cannot design clothes that look good on real women, why design clothes at all?"

"I love that," I tell him.

He smiles and leans back. "And it is because I love women. I truly love women—women of all shapes and sizes and colors." He holds up a finger. "It is my opinion that not all designers love women. I think some designers love their clothing more than they love their women."

"I think you're absolutely right," I say with enthusiasm. "Some designers see women as something to display their fashions on, like a coat hanger—not as real people with real lives and real needs."

"Ah, so you are the realist sister." He nods and turns to Paige. "And you are the romantic?"

"That's fairly accurate," Paige admits. "But we rub off on each other."

"Rub off?" He frowns.

"We influence each other," I say. "I try to get Paige to think more realistically and she tries to get me to loosen up."

He laughs. "Is a good combination."

We talk awhile longer, then, as promised, we end the interview within the hour. "Thank you so much for taking time to visit with us," Paige tells him. "I know our viewers are going to love hearing your thoughts on fashion."

"And on real women," I add.

We wrap it up and, as usual whenever we do these kinds of interviews, Alberto invites us to go with his assistant and do some "shopping" in his show room. "I would be proud to have my clothes worn by such lovely young women." He tips his head in a bow. "Now, if you will please excuse me."

"Alberto Baggatio is perfectly delightful," I say to Paige as we're leaving the studio. "I've become a real fan."

She chuckles. "I thought you'd like him."

Next we do the Nina Ricci show, arriving just in time to get our seats before the show begins. The styles remind me a bit of Rhiannon's designs, which I mention to Paige. "You're right," she says in surprise, like she can't believe I've been paying that much attention. And there is a similarity in the styles—the use of lace, ruffles, and other interesting feminine touches. The color scheme, except for pops of yellow, is rather neutral.

Afterward, Paige is able to get some words with chief designer Peter Copping. She compliments him on what seems to have been a highly successful show. And he opens up and tells her some of the thoughts behind his inspirations.

"Well, I think you're just brilliant," she tells him. "The way you carry on the Ricci tradition is superb. I'm sure Maria would be quite pleased."

He smiles as he thanks her. "And you will come to our after-party tonight?"

"We'll try to drop by," she says. "Thank you so much for taking time to speak to me."

He takes her hand and kisses it. "A pleasure."

As we walk away I quietly ask her if she got the name wrong. "Wasn't it *Nina* Ricci? I think you said Maria."

"Her name was also Maria—Nina was a nickname."

I nod. It figures Paige would know this.

Next we go to the Louis Vuitton show. A year ago, all I knew about Louis Vuitton was that the company made handbags and luggage. But watching the fashions on the runway today, I realize that this is a style I can embrace. In a way these styles are similar to Baggatio's; they seem like real clothes for real women. I see flowing skirts, fitted jackets, and quality fabrics—very classic and stylish. They remind me of some of the clothes my favorite old movie icons wore in the forties. I think I would enjoy wearing these clothes.

We only have time for some quick questions with their designer before we need to get over to Gucci to do our last interview of the day. The Gucci people are polite and helpful, but I can tell they are as eager to get this over with as we are. And Paige, probably distracted with the fact that Dylan is in town, wraps up the interview rather quickly.

"Another day, another dime," she says lightly as we go out to the car.

"You are taking this seriously, aren't you?" Mom quietly

questions Paige as Leah speaks to the driver about tomorrow's itinerary.

"Of course." Paige gives her an indignant look. "This is my show. I take it very seriously."

Mom looks skeptical. "Well, it seemed you rushed that last interview."

"Look, Mom." Paige stands up straighter. "I try to gauge my interviewees. If they're not interested or they're feeling rushed, it's not going to be a good interview anyway. Sometimes we just have to cut our losses and go. That one might not even make it on the show."

"But it's Gucci," Mom points out.

"So?" Paige narrows her eyes. "No offense, Mom. But I've been doing this longer than you and I think I know what I'm doing."

Mom glances at me and I just shrug. I can't disagree with Paige since she is very good at her job, but I see Mom's side too.

"We got a lot of good footage today," I say as we get into the car.

"We did," Paige agrees. Then she leans toward the driver, calling to him in broken Italian. "*Scusi*, can you drop me at Hotel Bulgari, *per favore*?"

"What for?" Mom asks.

Paige turns to her with a scowl. "To see Dylan."

"Oh." Mom nods, but I can tell she's not pleased.

"I'll have Dylan bring me back to the hotel in time to go to the after-parties," she says to us. "Erin can come with us after dinner if she wants."

I frown. "That's such a warm invitation, how can I resist?"

"Well, you don't usually like the after-parties anyway."

I shrug. "That's true."

"Maybe I'll go with Erin," Mom says.

Now I love my mom, but I'm not in love with the idea of having her as my date. Paige tosses me a look now, like maybe she feels a little guilty. "No, Mother," she says firmly. "Erin will come with Dylan and me. Right, Erin?"

"I guess."

Now I'm not sure which would be worse ... going with my mom or crashing my sister's date. Mostly I want to get out of going at all. But I decide to let it go for now. I can work it out later with Paige.

Chapter
13

"Is that someone you know?" Mom asks me as we're walking into the hotel.

"Huh?"

"Over there." She points to where a young man is hurrying toward us, waving to catch our attention.

"That's Gabin," I tell her as I wave back.

"Erin!" he exclaims as we hug. "I hoped you were here, but now I see you!" He holds me at arm's length and looks into my face. "You are more beautiful than I remember."

"Thanks." I feel my cheeks grow warm at this unexpected attention. "And your English has improved a lot."

He nods eagerly. "I have been practicing."

I turn and introduce him to Mom and Leah.

He smiles at my mom. "I see beauty runs in the family."

She laughs then pats him on the back. "I think I'm going to like you, Gabin." She gets this look in her eye—like she's up to something. "And I may be stepping over a line here, but I know that Erin isn't interested in tagging along with Paige and Dylan to the after-parties tonight."

Gabin frowns. "Tagging along?"

"Never mind," I say quickly.

Then his eyes light up. "You do not have a date tonight?"

I toss Mom a look. Leah just laughs.

"I am honored to escort you," Gabin says.

"What a great idea!" Mom exclaims.

"And so out of the blue," I tease.

"Is that mean yes?" Gabin asks hopefully.

I agree, but I suggest that we connect with Dylan and Paige as well, and he seems okay with that. "We can meet in the lobby," he says, "around, uh, eight?"

"Sounds perfect."

"Ciao!" He says with a grin.

"Ciao," I echo.

"What a sweet guy," Leah says as we get in the elevator.

"And attractive," my mom adds.

I tell them both about Gabin's connection to the Hermès family then explain to Leah how Gabin gave me my Birkin bag in Paris, and how Paige went crazy with jealousy when she didn't get one.

"Then he gave Erin another Birkin bag," Mom fills in. "A pink one for Paige."

"And then everyone was happy," I say as we part company to go into our rooms. Actually, the truth is that Gabin hadn't been happy that day, because I told him I wasn't ready for a relationship with him. Paige questioned me about it at the time, and in retrospect it seems a bit immature on my part. Really, what would've been wrong with continuing to be friends with a sweet guy like Gabin and seeing where things go? It's just that I was worried that he was more into me than I was into him, and I didn't want to hurt him. But maybe I over-thought it at the time. Perhaps I'll revisit it tonight.

Once I'm in my room, I check my iPhone. There's a text message from Mollie and one from Blake. I read Mollie's first. She's feeling bummed, missing me, and worried that she's not a good mommy. I text her back, saying she is a very good mommy and that I miss her too, and I gently ask if she needs to make an appointment with her counselor. She seemed to have turned a corner with the baby blues last month, but maybe she still needs some additional help.

Then I look at Blake's message, which isn't that different from the last one he sent. I write back, telling him we had a good day and that I'm going to the after-parties with Gabin tonight. Blake met Gabin in France, and at the time I thought he was jealous of Gabin. I'm curious how he'll react now . . . or if he'll react at all. And then I have to ask myself why I even care. Or maybe I don't. They say the heart is a fickle thing . . . and I'm starting to wonder if that's true.

As it turns out, Gabin and I don't cross paths with Dylan and Paige at the Nina Ricci after-party. But we do run into Taylor Mitchell and Eliza Wilton. I'm happy to see Taylor, but I feel awkward around Eliza. Still, I try to make polite conversation, asking them what they're doing in Milan this week.

"I'm on a research mission," Eliza laughs. "At least that's why the trip counts as a tax deduction."

I explain Eliza's new partnership to Gabin. "Did Rhiannon come?" I ask her hopefully.

"No, she's home, working. Maybe next year she'll get to come."

"So are you doing Dylan's show?" I ask Taylor.

Taylor's mouth twists slightly to one side. "No, I'm not doing much with Dylan these days."

"That's for sure." Eliza makes a sly smile, like she's holding back something really juicy. Maybe to hold Eliza off from gossiping, Taylor quickly explains how she's modeling for Versace this week. "The show's tomorrow." She sends Eliza what seems like a warning glance, like she wants her to keep her mouth shut. I wonder if it's because Taylor doesn't appreciate Eliza's recent publicity in regard to Dylan.

"Versace . . ." I say to Taylor. "That's impressive."

Her dark eyes sparkle. "Yes, I was impressed too. They approached me in Paris, but I didn't take them too seriously."

"Apparently they took you seriously."

She shrugs like it's not a big deal.

"So where's Paige tonight?" Eliza asks with a bit too much curiosity.

"She and Dylan were supposed to meet us here," I say casually.

"And how about my buddy JJ?" Taylor directs this to me. "I left him a message, inviting him to use my name to get in here tonight."

"I haven't seen him since this afternoon," I admit. "I can give him a call if you want."

"Oh, that's okay." We're joined by several others and the conversation hops around from topic to topic in a gossipy sort of way. But the way Taylor and Eliza reacted when I mentioned Dylan's name has me so distracted that I can't completely focus. So I simply study Eliza as she interacts in her usual chatterbox way, making her life seem larger and more important than I suspect it really is. Suddenly I'm worried that Eliza might not be finished with her pursuit of my sister's fiancée just yet.

"So where's the lovely Paige Forrester?" one of the Ricci stylists asks me. "We hoped we'd see her tonight."

"She's supposed to be here." I repeat what I said earlier then I compliment him on the Ricci show today. "It felt really fresh, and so feminine too." I'm tempted to bring up Rhiannon and how I think she has a style that's complementary to Ricci's spring line, but I suspect that's not an appropriate thing to say.

Instead I turn to Gabin, asking him if he wants to go check out the food table with me. Mostly I want to escape this little throng of gregarious fashion freaks. Okay, I suppose they're not really freaks. I just feel the need for a break from all this.

"I'm kind of worried about Paige and Dylan," I confess to Gabin after we've both gleaned some tasty-looking appetizers and are off on the sidelines, balancing our plates and drinks, nibbling our food, and watching the colorful crowd.

"What is wrong?" he asks me.

I think about this. "Can I trust you, Gabin?"

He smiles. "You know you can, Erin."

And I know this is true. Gabin is just like that. "Maybe you heard about the rumored affair between Eliza and Dylan? It was in some of the tabloids."

He nods somberly. "Yes, I read something on an online fashion site. I hoped it was just that—a rumor."

"I hoped so too. But something about the way Eliza is acting tonight ... well, it has me worried."

"You are very loyal to your sister." Gabin takes a sip of champagne.

I shrug. "She's my sister."

He presses his lips together then glances off to the side, like there's something he wants to say, but can't.

"Do you think it's wrong that I'm concerned for my sister's interests?" I ask him.

"No. But what of your own interests, Erin?"

"Oh." I nod. "Good point."

"Perhaps ... it seems your sister ... she is demanding of your attention."

I can't help but laugh.

"She is a grown woman, Erin. She must live her life. She must make her mistakes."

"Yes, I know you're right. But part of my job is to watch out for her." I explain how Helen calls me Jiminy Cricket sometimes, which makes Gabin chuckle.

"Oh, yes, I remember Pinocchio and the little cricket." His eyes light up. "And Pinocchio." He taps the side of his head. "He was not too smart. He needed a cricket to help him."

"And Paige?"

He smiles. "She is a smart one. But perhaps ... she doesn't always make the same decision as you. No?"

"That's for sure."

He gets a thoughtful look. "I do not like to criticize."

"Criticize?" I frown. *"Me?"*

He shakes his head. "No, not you."

"Paige?"

"No ... not Paige. It is not my place to be suspicious. I like you and I like your sister."

"And ...?" I wait.

"And ... *Dylan Marceau* ... I am not so sure."

"Not so sure about what?"

"I do not know if he is who your sister thinks he is."

"I don't understand."

"Dylan is not so unusual—he is a man who loves his beautiful women. Sometimes he perhaps ... loves them *too much*."

Suddenly the appetizers are not so appetizing. In fact, it feels like there's a brick in the pit of my stomach. "Do you know this for sure?"

"I have heard Dylan talk, Erin. The way men talk sometimes ... around other men."

"Oh ..." I nod slowly. I get it. "Was that before Dylan and Paige were engaged?"

"Yes. Perhaps he has changed?"

"Perhaps."

Gabin makes a stiff smile. "Like I said, I do not like to criticize. But I say this because of your concern."

We put our plates away and do some more mingling. Then I decide to pay a visit to the little girls' room before we head on over to the Louis Vuitton after-party, where I'm hoping to find Paige.

"Erin," Taylor says as I'm emerging from the restroom. "Do you have a minute?"

"Sure." I smile. "What's up?"

She guides me over to a settee by a big marble column. "I'm not good at beating around the bush," she begins.

"Huh?"

"I know you've heard the rumors about Dylan and Eliza. Rhiannon filled me in on how Paige confronted Eliza while you were filming for your show, which by the way, I think was a brilliant strategy."

"It did turn out rather well. I think." I frown.

"And you probably noticed Eliza acting a bit suspicious earlier."

"I kind of wondered what was up. Is she still involved with Dylan?"

"No. At least I don't think so. There's a reason I quit working for Dylan, Erin. And Rhiannon accidentally spilled this to Eliza, just a couple of days ago. And, as you know, Eliza has a big mouth."

"I'm not sure I'm following you."

"Dylan has always been friendly with me," Taylor says in an offhanded way. "I'm used to that kind of attention . . . and I know how to deal with it. But when he continued, you know, being so attentive—after he was engaged to Paige, well, I just got tired of it. So I quit."

"So Dylan was coming on to you?" I ask. "Even though he was engaged?"

"I wish it weren't true. You know, despite his weaknesses in regard to women, I really do like Dylan. He gave me my first break in modeling."

"So why are you telling me?"

Taylor makes a sympathetic face. "I know it's a lot to unload on you, Erin. And I also know how close you and Paige are. I know how protective you are of her. And, well, I just couldn't say this to Paige, but I'm worried Eliza might let it slip out. In fact, she might have already. I warned her not to say anything, but controlling Eliza is like controlling the weather."

I let out an exasperated sigh, trying to wrap my head around this. "So . . . can I ask you something?"

"Sure. Go for it."

"Do you think Dylan loves Paige?"

She nods. "I *know* he loves her."

I consider this. "But does he love her enough to be true to her? Or is she just one of his favorite loves?"

Taylor's mouth twists to one side. "I wish I could say that Dylan will be true to Paige. The truth is, I don't know. And I'm sorry to say this, but if I were Paige, I wouldn't trust him."

"Right ..."

She gives me a side hug. "I'm sorry to dump this on you, Erin. But I'm glad you're a Christian, because I know you'll handle it the right way."

"The right way?"

She chuckles. "I know, it's not always obvious. What I mean is, I'm sure you'll figure it out. And, who knows, maybe Eliza won't say anything. Just the same, I hate to see Paige get hurt. She doesn't deserve it."

"But she is a big girl," I say. "And sometimes when I try to intervene, it goes sideways."

"Yeah, I know. I guess it's like my grandmother used to say."

"What's that?"

"A word to the wise is sufficient." She smiles.

"Thanks," I tell her. Just then we see JJ coming toward us with Gabin. Taylor lights up when she sees JJ, and the four of us decide to share a taxi to the next after-party. Although I try not to obsess over what Taylor just told me, and I'm trying to balance her news against Gabin's advice for me to take a step back in Paige's life, it's hard not to feel sad for my sister. I hope we can finish Milan Fashion Week before anything serious hits the fan.

Chapter
14

In the morning we get to attend a very cool photo shoot that is actually on the roof of Milan Cathedral. Naturally, we remain along the sidelines, but our camera guys get some amazing footage and Paige and I nab some quick behind-the-scenes interviews with some top Italian models.

"Duomo di Milano is one of the world's largest churches," Paige says into our cameras. "And as you can see, it's quite spectacular up here." She waves to the rows of spires that line two sides of the roof.

"Actually, this cathedral is second in size only to Saint Peter's Basilica in Rome," I tell the camera. "But unlike Saint Peter's, this cathedral, which was started in the late fourteenth century, has been under construction ever since."

"Talk about job security," Paige jokes. "Think of all the generations of builders who spent their entire lives working on this."

"It's definitely beautiful," I say.

"Speaking of beautiful"—Paige nods to a model who's waiting for some camera time—"I want to introduce our viewers to the stunning Bianca Balti." She does a quick interview with this long-legged dark beauty and then waves another one over. "This is Elisabetta Canalis," she says. "Some might remember her appearance in *Deuce Bigalow*. Haven't you been in some other films as well, Elisabetta?"

Elisabetta lists some other projects she's been involved in, and then it's her turn to pose for some still shots on the photogenic rooftop. Finally it's time for us to wrap it up here and head over to the first fashion show of the day. I feel a little nervous because I know this is the Versace show—and that Taylor Mitchell will be modeling in it today. However, as far as I can tell, Paige hasn't heard any of the Taylor and Dylan rumors ... yet.

"You girls didn't say much about last night's after-parties," Leah says as we're riding over to the Versace show.

"They were great," Paige tells her. "But Erin and I must've gotten our wires crossed. She went to the Ricci one first and Dylan and I went to the Louis Vuitton one."

"So we were like ships in the night," I say lightly. The truth is, I'm not even sure if Paige and Dylan attended the parties. At least Paige made it back to our suite last night ... or early this morning. So far I haven't had a private conversation with her, which is kind of a relief since I have no idea what I'd say—or if I'd even say anything about what Taylor told me. And I can tell, based on her cheerful demeanor, that she hasn't had a conversation with Eliza yet. Hopefully she won't.

"This is an evening-gown show," Paige says as we're getting out. "I heard Taylor Mitchell will be in it. I want to see if I can get her for a behind-the-scenes chat."

"I'm sure JJ will like that," I say as we wave to our guys, who are just getting out of the van ahead of us.

We show our passes and head back into the staging area, where Paige quickly spots Taylor and waves her over to us. I see Taylor toss me a curious glance, but the girl's as cool as a cucumber as she walks over to Paige, wearing a stunning red gown with cutouts on the sides.

"Versace is known for its beautiful models," Paige is saying into the camera as Taylor joins us, "but Taylor Mitchell is one of the hottest new commodities in the fashion world." She grins at Taylor. "I know for a fact that she's so hot, Versace snatched her away from my fiancé, Dylan Marceau." She makes a pouty face to Taylor. "Surely you'll come back and do some more modeling for the Marceau line someday?"

Taylor smiles. "You never know. And I always say, don't burn your bridges."

"Smart girl." Paige gestures to her dress. "And that is absolutely stunning, Taylor. Can you turn around?"

Taylor does a graceful turn. "I just love Versace," she says into the hand mic. "I didn't grow up like some of the models here, dreaming of becoming a supermodel. But I know enough about fashion to appreciate Versace. I couldn't believe it when I was invited to Milan."

"Well, Versace is lucky to get you, Taylor." Paige smiles in a way that assures me, and probably Taylor too, that she truly is oblivious to any new rumors. "And we won't take any more of your time. Have a good show!"

Paige moves on to another model. She's a stunning blonde who seems eager to get in a few words. Then we hear the music increasing in tempo and we know it's time to go find our seats.

"This should be a gorgeous show," Paige says as we sit down.

"Yes." I nod as if I'm really into it, but mostly I'm just thankful that so far the day has been business as usual. I hope the pattern continues. The show, as expected, is one of the best—all is perfection and the models are incredibly beautiful. I mean beautiful in a healthy sort of way. Their skin glows and they are not skeletons. I decide that I like Versace.

Our next event is Emporio Armani menswear, but we don't make it in time to do any behind-the-scenes interviews before the show. And this show is actually a refreshing change from the women's shows. It starts with a shirtless guy on a bright-blue unicycle, doing tricks up and down the runway. The music is surprisingly low key, almost quiet, and then a parade of gorgeous men strut out dressed in everything from shorts to suits. One guy is wearing what looks like a prison outfit. The spirit is fun and light … and the men are hot. Then it ends with a bunch of shirtless guys on brightly colored unicycles, which creates a circus atmosphere that I find very entertaining.

After the show, Paige has a good time interviewing the male models. The guys are in good spirits, I think the celebratory champagne has already started to flow, and they all seem more than willing to cooperate with her questions. Finally I remind her that we still have the Hermès show to attend, so we tell the guys ciao and head on our way.

"You seem very eager to get to the Hermès show on time," she says in a teasing tone. "Does it have anything to do with a certain French guy?"

I haven't really had a chance to talk to Paige much, so I'm surprised she knows about Gabin.

"I filled her in." Mom makes a knowing smile as we walk toward the car.

"So how is old Gabin these days?" Paige continues.

"He seems well." As we walk, I'm thinking about Gabin's careful advice to me last night in regard to Paige—not that I plan to let on. "He asked how you were doing."

"He's such a gentleman."

"He certainly is," Mom agrees. "I was impressed."

"And that reminds me, you girls got an official invite to the Hermès after-party tonight," Leah says. "I'm sure Gabin must've set that up."

"There's also the Versace party," Paige says. "I told Dylan I'd go to that one with him."

"Maybe you girls can get your plans coordinated tonight," Mom suggests.

I'm about to protest this, thinking I wouldn't mind having some space between Paige and me again tonight. Or maybe it's Dylan I want to avoid. But Paige acts like this is a great idea.

"That sounds like fun," she tells me. "Let's try to leave together from the hotel tonight and stick together for both parties. I'm sure Dylan would enjoy spending some time with Gabin again. Those two really seemed to hit it off in France. Remember?"

"Yeah." I nod, but I'm getting that heavy feeling again. I know Gabin's fine European upbringing will help him to act the perfect gentleman, but what if I can't act civilly toward Dylan?

We've barely entered the room where the Hermès show is scheduled when Gabin comes over, warmly greeting us. Thankfully, he doesn't do or say a thing to hint to Paige what he knows. Not that I expected him to, but I'm still relieved.

"We're going to double date with you tonight," she chirps at him.

"Double date?" He looks confused and I suddenly realize how embarrassing this could turn. Gabin hasn't even asked me out and here we are conspiring.

"Wait," I say to Paige. "It's likely that Gabin has other plans. This is a busy time for him and it's—"

"What do you mean?" Gabin looks at me. "Are you inviting me to be your date again tonight?"

"*I'm* inviting you," Paige says coaxingly.

"To escort *you*?" he asks with bewilderment, "or Erin?"

She laughs. "Erin, of course."

He smiles at me. "I would be honored."

"And a double date means all four of us will go out together," she explains. "You and Erin, and Dylan and me. Maybe you and Dylan can arrange to meet at the hotel."

His brows arch slightly. "Oh. *That* is a double date. I see."

I exchange a glance with him, and I could be wrong, but I think he understands this is not going to be easy for me.

"We will make it a memorable night," he tells us.

"And now we'd like to get some interviews behind the scenes," she tells him. "If you don't mind."

"No, we are expecting you."

The camera guys are ready, so we head back to the staging area where Paige starts to interview a French supermodel that Gabin already selected for us. I pull Alistair over to where I'm standing and do an impromptu interview with Gabin, asking him questions about Hermès, what direction they're going, and so on.

"Not everyone knows that Hermès has a clothing line," I say to him. "Some of our viewers might assume you're only about scarves and bags."

"It is true, we are well-known for our leather and accessories," he says, "but Hermès is more than just that."

"Can you tell us a bit about your spring line?"

And so he explains what to expect for spring, talking about colors and styles with the expertise of a designer who respects women and truly loves fashion.

As I'm winding it down, Gabin grins at me. "You have become an excellent interviewer, Erin."

"Better than in Paris?" I tease.

He nods. "Perhaps you have grown in many ways."

I feel another warm rush to my cheeks. I turn to Alistair, telling him I think that's enough for now, and suggest he might collect some candid footage before the show starts.

"And now we must get ready for the big event," Gabin says in a businesslike way. *"Au revoir, mon cheri."*

"Au revoir," I say back to him. As I walk away I wonder, what girl doesn't get a rush from hearing a real Frenchman speaking French?

I wait for Paige to wrap up her interview with a Yugoslavian model who looks like she could use a good meal, and we make our way to our seats. I still get a little thrill when I see our names printed on the placards marking our chairs, usually in the front row. It really is an honor; I think perhaps the more I learn about this industry, the more I appreciate it.

Hermès is not disappointing. The drama, the fashions, the models, the music, the setting, the lights . . . all are *très chic, très France*. I am reminded of all the things I love about Parisian fashion. It seems that femininity is making a comeback with many of the couture collections this season, and I must admit it's refreshing to see. Not that I've ever been into ruffles and frills, but there is something reassuring about these classic styles. Call me old-fashioned, but I like it when a dress looks like a dress and not something someone should be wearing as they journey into space.

"Well, that was a good day's work," Paige says as we're trooping back to where the car should be picking us up.

"And you girls were great today," Leah tells us.

"They seem to know what they're doing," Mom observes.

Paige laughs. "Well, let's hope so. By now you'd think we should've learned a thing or two."

"Tomorrow afternoon is Dylan's show," Mom says as we get into the car. "But first we have some shops to visit. We're scheduled to visit Gucci, Armani, Valentino, Fendi, and Prada." She shakes her head. "I can barely imagine."

Paige claps her hands. *"Fantastico! Non vedo l'ora!"*

"What's that mean?" I ask her.

"I cannot wait."

"Can you say shop until you drop in Italian?" Leah asks.

"Hmm ... shop is *negozio,*" she says. "Like negotiate."

Mom pulls out her little English-to-Italian handbook and as we ride to the hotel, we try to figure out how to say some goofy phrases.

"Mangeremo pasta," Mom finally says as our car pulls up to the hotel.

"Let's eat pasta?" Paige guesses.

"Yes. Since Leah and I don't get invited to your fancy after-parties, how about if we all go to dinner together first?"

"Great idea," I say. "The food always looks yummy at the parties, but it's usually difficult to actually eat."

"I'll see if the concierge can make a reservation for us," Leah offers.

Once we're in our suite, while Paige is getting a shower, I

check my phone messages. One from Mollie sounds like she's perked up a bit since yesterday. To my disappointment there's nothing from Blake, and so I send him nothing. But I can't help but wonder, what is he doing? Is he with Grace? Am I losing him? And then I get irritated with myself for even thinking like this. What is coming over me? Would I really want a relationship that was motivated by jealousy? Of course not.

Dinner is amazing—so many kinds of pasta! Naturally, we all eat too much. Well, except for Paige. She, as usual, seems to be watching her waistline. It's ironic since she is by far the thinnest of the four of us. To make up for pigging out we decide to walk back to the hotel, which turns out to be about a mile.

"No one told me we were going on a hike tonight," Paige complains. "I would've worn different shoes."

"Do you want me to wave down a taxi?" Leah offers.

"No," Mom tells her. "I can see the hotel from here."

And so we trudge on. Mom and Leah take the lead and I hang back with Paige. "Are you getting blisters?" I ask.

"I hope not. But, really, this was nuts. I was tempted to call Dylan to come get us and just head to the parties, except I want to change my clothes first."

To distract her, and get the topic away from Dylan, I talk about tomorrow's shopping expedition. I ask her which shop she's most into. But as we're discussing Prada's new line of fall boots, I'm really thinking about Dylan Marceau ... and how I know he's going to break my sister's heart. I wonder how she can be so oblivious.

Chapter
15

As usual, Paige is in charge of wardrobe as we dress for the after-parties. It doesn't take long for her to decide that I "must" wear the garnet-colored Gucci cocktail dress. I don't argue. It's a good style, not too short, not too low cut, but very pretty—and like Paige says, garnet is a good color for me. And the matching shoes she picks for me to wear with it are perfect. "You make style seem so simple," I tell her as I check out my image in the mirror.

"Sometimes." She shakes her head as she goes through the rack of clothes again. For some reason, she's having a harder time finding a dress for herself tonight. Finally, she is standing in front of the mirror, wearing the kind of gorgeous, lacy underwear that makes me nervous, as she holds up a creamy satin dress. It's so elegant and beautiful, I can't believe it when she hangs it back up in the closet.

"Why aren't you wearing that?" I demand. "It looks fabulous."

"I'm saving it for tomorrow night."

"What's tomorrow night?"

"The House of Marceau after-party," she says with pride.

"Oh ... is that going to be a big shindig?"

She shrugs. "Well, not by Gucci standards, but it will be a big night for Dylan and me. I want to look my best for him."

She holds up a little black dress. "I could go the safe route tonight."

I frown. "But you're Paige Forrester," I remind her. "You're supposed to make heads turn when you enter the room."

She laughs. "Yes, but that's what everyone's trying to do at these parties. If I go with this Valentino classic, I might just stand out for being the only one there in a little black dress."

"You're the expert."

She frowns at the clock. "And we're running out of time."

I spot a gold dress in the back of the closet. "Hey, what about this one?" I ask as I hold it up to the light where it sparkles with promise.

Her eyes light up. *"Versace!"*

"You think it will work?"

"Oh, Erin, it's perfect. I totally forgot about that dress. And one of the parties is Versace. You're a genius."

Feeling lucky, while she's slipping into the dress I scramble through the shoes, finally choosing a pair of gold metallic sandals with killer high heels. "What about—"

"Perfect," she cries as she grabs them. "We'll both be wearing Prada shoes tonight."

I bite my tongue as I watch her trying accessories. I don't want to get in an argument with her right now, but I do have some questions about Prada's environmental and global practices. However, I know Paige loves their designs, so really what's the point? Maybe that's the attitude I need to adopt with her love life too—kind of a don't-ask, don't-tell policy. She tries this and that until she finally decides on a fairly simple pair of gold and pearl earrings. The effect is perfect. "Here," she says as she hands me some twisted silver earrings. "These will look dramatic with that dress." She holds up a necklace. "And I think you need this too."

I try it on and decide, once again, she is right. "Thanks for the help," I tell her as we make final adjustments to our makeup. Then, as we're selecting the right evening bags, her phone rings.

"We're on our way down," she chirps happily.

"Thank you," she tells me as she does some last-minute preening in the mirror by the elevator. "I totally forgot about this Versace—and it's absolute perfection." She then looks slightly dismayed. "I wonder if I should've saved it for tomorrow night."

"No time now," I say as we get into the elevator. "And you will definitely turn heads in that."

"As long as I turn Dylan's head."

I nod, biting my tongue. Suddenly I'm thankful that I found such an incredibly fabulous dress for Paige to wear tonight. The Versace *is* stunning. For some reason I think she might need it. I don't even know why exactly, but I want my sister to be at her very best. I want her to stand tall and regal, no matter what comes her way. Even as I think this, I hope nothing too terrible comes her way. I've seen her derailed before, and it's not pretty. Besides that, we still have five more days of shooting to do. I know I can go solo, but I don't want to.

As we walk through the lobby, we are noticed. And it's not like that happens easily during Fashion Week. This is a tough crowd. But Paige is dazzling. Next to her ... well, I'm probably invisible. The guys wave to us from where they're waiting by the fireplace.

"*Buonasera,*" Gabin says as he takes my hand. "*Sei bellissima.*"

I giggle. "Thanks. Your Italian is as good as your French."

"No, not even close. But I try." He kisses my hand.

Out of the corner of my eye, I watch Dylan greeting Paige with a long, passionate kiss on the lips. "You look lovely," he says as he possessively links her hand over his arm, almost as if she's his prize ... or maybe wrist candy. I don't like to feel this way, but I'm aggravated. I think Dylan is a big fat phony and the sooner it blows wide open, the better it might be for everyone. The thought makes my stomach clench with anxiety.

"Are you okay?" Gabin asks quietly. He's peering at me almost as if he can see right through me. "All ready to go now?"

I force a smile and will my feet to move. "Sure." I look more carefully at Gabin, actually seeing him for the first time. "And you look very handsome tonight," I say as we head out to where Dylan and Paige are already entering the waiting car.

"You are worried about Paige?" he says discreetly.

I nod. "I'm trying to follow your advice. It's just not easy." I haven't even told him about what Taylor said to me outside the restroom last night, how she confirmed his suspicions about Dylan's attraction to beautiful women. But I have a feeling I don't need to tell Gabin this. I suspect he might know even more than he's let on.

We get into the limo and Paige begins to chatter away, telling all about what we did and saw today. She is like the quintessential charming talk show hostess—watch out, Kelly Ripa. With Paige in top form there is never a dull moment, never a lull in conversation. She is clever and funny, gifted at making others feel important, and liberal in her praise as she compliments her fiancée on his spring line. Dylan is eating it up.

"You're being awfully quiet tonight," Dylan says to me suddenly. "What's wrong? Aren't you enjoying your time in Milan?"

I make a stiff smile. "I adore Milan," I tell him. "Almost as much as I love Paris."

Gabin looks hopefully at me. "You prefer Paris to Milan?"

"I'm not positive … I mean, I haven't seen all that much of Milan," I admit. "To be fair, it's a bit like comparing apples to oranges. But *maybe* I prefer Paris."

"*Splendide!*" Gabin looks somewhat victorious. "I always know you have excellent taste, Erin."

"Don't get me wrong. Milan is totally amazing. I love the architecture. And the food is awesome. Really, it's a beautiful city too."

"And tomorrow we go shopping!" Paige sighs happily. "Millions of girls would kill to have my job." She beams at Dylan. "*And* my life."

"Maybe we should get you a good life insurance policy," I tease. But I'm thinking there probably are a few women out there, the Elizas of this world, who wouldn't mind seeing Paige snuffed out.

Somehow we make it through the night and both afterparties, visiting with the who's who of the fashion world without hitting any serious bumps along the way. I get a little nervous when Paige insists on inviting Taylor and JJ to join us at the Versace party, but Taylor acts perfectly normal. And, thankfully, Eliza must be elsewhere. I don't even ask. I don't want to know.

When the evening finally comes to an end, I am hugely relieved. I feel like my sister is sitting on a time bomb, and yet she has no idea. As we go up to our suite a bit before one in the morning, I have to ask myself, what does a loyal and loving sister do in this situation?

According to Gabin, *nothing*. According to Taylor ... well, even she was a little fuzzy on it. She acted as if my faith was somehow going to get me through this dilemma. And suddenly, I realize I haven't even prayed about the situation.

"You really did seem extra quiet tonight," Paige tells me as we're getting ready for bed. "Is something wrong?"

I think hard, wondering if this is my opportunity to lay the cards on the table, spell it all out for her. But somehow I know that's not the right thing to do just yet.

"I think I'm just tired," I tell her. And this is true. As I go to bed, I decide there's no way I can bring any of this up to Paige before I've asked for God's help. I need some special spiritual direction and discernment for this. I need to pray. So that's what I do. Before I go to sleep, I pray long and hard for Paige. I even pray for Dylan. Really, for all I know, he could be more innocent than I've been led to think. In all fairness, I haven't heard his side yet. You can't convict someone based on rumors.

The next morning starts out the same as usual: Shawna and Luis show up and go to work on us, Paige picks out our wardrobe, and then we head out to shop.

"Okay, girls," Mom says as we're riding in the car, "we don't want it to look like you're speed shopping, but to stay on schedule and hit all the shops we've put on the docket, you will have to spend an average of only twenty minutes in each shop. Can you do that?"

"It won't be easy," Paige admits.

"I'll watch for your cues," I promise.

As Mom continues briefing us about how much to spend, which is a crazy amount of money, I can't help think of how unrealistic these portions of our "reality" show really are. I mean, seriously, how many girls wake up to a hair stylist and cosmetologist, get to wear expensive designer clothes, and are chauffeured off to some of the most highfalutin shops on the planet and told to shop until they drop or the studio's American Express card melts down or maxes out? It's ridiculous.

Yet here we are, shopping at Gucci like we're made of money. Okay, the truth is we do have a budget. But it's also true that some of the shops offer discounts in exchange for promotion on our show. We pay visits to Armani and Valentino, pause for espressos, then head on to Fendi and finally Prada — where Paige is in hog heaven. Okay, she wouldn't appreciate that metaphor, but it works for me.

Part of our "on the town" show includes us having lunch at a traditional Milan trattoria. Naturally, they're expecting us, but because the space is small, we only take in one camera. Mom and Leah get a table near the kitchen, but Paige and I are seated at one of the small tables in a more prestigious spot. Our waiter makes a great to-do about us and then we are presented with an antipasti plate of prosciutto and other meats, cheeses, and olives, "Complimentary!" This is followed by zuppa, gnocchi, and all the specialties of the house, until it's time for dessert and coffee.

"Now I'm ready for a nap," I say to Mom and Leah as we're getting back into the town car.

"That was scrumptious," Mom says as she checks her watch. "But no time for a nap. We have the Rosso show at two."

"And the Marceau show at four," Paige says happily.

"Rosso?" I say, trying to remember. "Is that the guy who designed the Eco Shoe?"

Paige laughs. "No, silly. Renzo Rosso is the designer behind Diesel."

"Right." I nod. "I knew that."

I try not to fall asleep during the Rosso show. Not that it's boring, because it's definitely not, but I've found out it's unwise to pork out on too much Italian food in the middle of the day. Now I realize that Paige is smart to eat small portions, not only for her figure's sake.

After the show we go backstage to get some behind-the-scenes footage that we arrived too late to shoot earlier. Fortunately, there's an espresso machine and I help myself to a small cup, hoping it will jar me back into action. It's a lively bunch back here, and we're getting some good interviews. But suddenly Mom is waving at us, saying it's time to get to the next show.

"Oh, great!" Paige exclaims as we're rushing to wrap it up. "Now I'm going to be late to Dylan's show."

She continues to complain as we get stuck in traffic. By the time we get to the Marceau show, we are indeed late. At least our seats are still waiting for us. We rush in as a model is strutting down the runway.

"Don't worry," I whisper in Paige's ear. "We can stay afterward for as long as you want. This is our last gig of the day."

At first she frowns at me, but she must've remembered that others might be watching. So she squares her shoulders, pastes a satisfied smile on her face, crosses her long legs, and focuses her attention on the runway.

My eyes are on the runway too. But I'm thinking—and

I could be wrong—that although the models are totally gorgeous and the music is great, the clothing is uniformly unimpressive. Oh, it's not terrible, and I certainly am no expert, but in my opinion it's rather ho-hum compared to what we've seen in Milan.

I sit up straighter and tell myself to pay better attention. I must be delusional or I'm still drowsy from too much lunch. Or maybe I'm being extra critical of Dylan because I suspect he's really a jerk. I blink and clear my thoughts and then stare at the beautiful blonde strutting by us in a pink-and-gray plaid jacket and skirt. It's similar to what I've seen Paige wear ... in the past. Something about it feels so last year to me.

And we're talking about *me*, not my fashion-forward sister. I could be imagining this, but I'm thinking Dylan Marceau might very well be, in the fashion world at least, *yesterday's news*. Because if anyone asked me—and there's a distinct possibility that could happen—I would have to say Dylan Marceau's new spring line is only so-so, run-of-the-mill, average. *Oh, my!*

Chapter
16

When Dylan's show ends, he comes out to make his appearance. Most of the designers do this, but I've noticed that they all do it a little differently. Ironically, it seems to have little to do with whether or not their designs are well-received. I've seen crowds with so much enthusiasm that it feels like the building might collapse, and then some iconic designer, say, Ralph Lauren, will make a quick appearance, bow, and then disappear—like it's no big deal.

At other times, when a crowd is politely clapping and people are making quick exits, I've seen lesser designers bow and make speeches and generally come off as narcissistic fools. Unfortunately, Dylan Marceau is falling into the latter category today. And when he calls for Paige to join him on the runway, I can tell by her expression that she is less than eager.

But being a lady, she does join him. He takes her hand and they both bow, which I'm sure must be making her feel like an idiot since this crowd seems to be of the politely clapping variety and already I see a lot of empty seats. But Paige is giving a full smile, and I wonder if perhaps I'm wrong or even jaded. Maybe she thinks Dylan's spring line is the best thing since Louboutin's red soles. That doesn't explain the crowd's response, however.

I go to where Leah and Mom are, as expected, on the sidelines. "What did you think?" I say quietly in Mom's ear. She gives me a curious expression, as if she's not sure how to answer. "Anyway," I continue, "I told Paige that since we got here late, we should probably stay as long as she likes to get some more behind-the-scenes footage." I think it's going to be a giant waste of time, because I seriously doubt that any of it will make it onto our show. At least I hope not.

Paige is coming over to us, still smiling. I can't tell if it's a shocked smile or if she's truly pleased. "So," I say carefully to her, "do you still want to get some more film?"

"Of course," she says cheerfully. She waves to the crew and we begin to make our way through the quickly dwindling crowd. I'm tempted to pop a mic in front of some of the spectators to get their reaction, but it might be too embarrassing. They probably know who I am and that my sister, Paige Forrester, star of *On the Runway* and the Queen of Style, is engaged to this uninspired designer.

Instead, I trail behind Paige, listening as she talks to the models and stylists. But even they seem a little unenthusiastic, and I suspect they know they have a bust on their hands. Even though they can always work for someone else, it must be difficult to act like all is well after a show like that.

I can tell I'm useless to Paige right now. I'm sure she wouldn't even want to hear my comments, since she seems determined to keep on her sunny face, acting like it was a fabulous show. She reminds me of the foolish king in the fairy tale "The Emperor's New Clothes." Anyway, I'm thirsty and I know there has to be a cooler of bottled water somewhere around here, so I wander into a vacated area that appears to have been used for hairstyling. Just as I'm plucking a bottle from a tub of melted ice, I hear a shuffling sound.

I peer over to see a couple, partially hidden behind a folding screen and oblivious to me, caught up in a passionate embrace. The brunette woman, obviously one of the models, is facing me, but her eyes are closed. It's not so unusual to catch people in "compromising positions" in this industry, but I feel embarrassed. Before I turn away, however, I recognize the dark gray suit and realize that the guy with his hands all over the girl is none other than my future brother-in-law!

I gasp, dropping the bottle of water with a loud clunk, which Dylan hears. He turns toward me and we lock eyes, and without saying a word, maybe not even breathing, I dash out of there. I return to where Paige is still talking to a model and breathlessly ask her if we should wrap it up now.

"What's wrong with you?" she asks, keeping her TV smile in place, although her eyes are curious. "You look like you just saw a ghost."

"Maybe I did," I tell her. "The ghost of fashion future."

She actually laughs. "*Really?* It seems more likely you'd see the ghost of fashion present. Or perhaps even fashion past. Maybe you saw Gianni Versace. You know he was tragically murdered, and I've heard that he shows up at some of the Milan shows." Her brow creases like she's thinking. "Actually, that would make a very interesting segment." She turns to Alistair's camera. "What do you think, fashion friends? How about a segment on the ghosts of fashion past?" She grins at me. "*Brilliant!*"

"I'll be with Mom and Leah," I tell her.

She looks as though she's about to question this, but I don't stick around. I feel sick to my stomach and I don't think it's from lunch.

"What's up?" Mom asks as I join her.

"Don't ask," I mutter.

"What?"

"Later," I mumble.

"Is Paige wrapping it up?" Leah asks.

"I wish she would," I moan. "I want to go home. I mean to the hotel."

"What is wrong with you?" Mom persists.

"My stomach hurts," I tell her as I see Dylan coming out. With what looks like a very fake smile, he begins mingling with the models and the few stragglers who have stuck around, likely making small talk as he's glancing about nervously. He's probably curious as to whether or not I've broken the news to Paige yet. Maybe he plans to do damage control. But I don't plan to stick around and see it. Instead I turn to Mom, telling her I'll be in the car.

"What is going—"

"Never mind," I seethe before storming away.

By the time I hear the car door opening, I'm somewhat cooled off and rational again. Oh, I don't know what I'll do or say just yet, but I know I won't sit by silently anymore. Mom and Leah get in, but Paige isn't with them. "Where's Paige?" I ask.

"She's going with Dylan," Mom says as Leah instructs the driver to take us to our hotel.

"*With Dylan?*" I demand.

"Yes." Mom nods and looks curiously at me. "Our work is done for the day and he wants her to help with the after-party."

I roll my eyes. "I'm sure he does."

"What's that supposed to mean?"

I bite my lip, uncertain of how much to say. It's one thing to spill the beans to Paige—after all, it's *her* life. And I wouldn't even mind telling Mom. But I'm not convinced Leah needs to hear all this. Not just yet anyway. Really, I need to talk to Paige first.

"What's wrong?" Leah presses me. "Why are you so upset?"

I shrug. "I don't feel very well."

"You seem angry, Erin." Mom studies me.

"I'm just tired," I tell her. And to change the subject I ask them what they thought of Dylan's spring line.

"It was nice," Mom says cautiously.

"It didn't seem quite as impressive as some of the others," Leah admits.

"I thought it was surprisingly ordinary," I tell them. "Borderline boring."

"Really?" Mom frowns at me. "That seems a bit harsh."

"It's the truth," I snap back.

"Sorry to say this." Leah looks uneasy. "I agree with Erin."

I launch into a critique that's not so dissimilar to how Paige will tear into a designer she thinks needs to find a new line of work. And perhaps it's a bit more cruel and heartless than necessary, but considering what I just witnessed, I don't particularly care.

At the hotel I tell Mom and Leah to go out to dinner if they like. "I'll order in if I get hungry, which is unlikely."

"Are you sick?" Mom looks worried.

"No," I assure her. "I just need some time to myself ... some space. Okay?"

She nods. She knows me well enough to know this is

sometimes spot-on true. I get worn out by crowds and busyness and new things. "Sure, honey," she says. "Just go up there and take it easy. Call me if you need anything."

"Okay," I promise as I give her a quick hug. Then I go directly to my suite, close the door, and just sit and stare out the window. I have no idea what I should do. I could try to call Paige, but how do I tell her something like this on the phone? Especially when I know she's with Dylan? And for all I know she'll be coming here to change for the party. Really, I decide, all I can do is wait. And pray.

After I've prayed, I check my iPhone. Once again, the only messages are from Mollie, but I text her back and without going into detail, I ask her to pray for Paige, saying it's urgent. Out of habit, I want to text Blake too, but I'm slightly irked, and mostly hurt, that he hasn't been in touch. I hate to assume this is because of Grace, but part of me feels that's a reasonable explanation. Probably even more so after witnessing Dylan's despicable behavior this afternoon.

Even so, I'm tempted to text Blake anyway. After all, we are friends, and he's Paige's friend too. And he's prayed for me in the past. But before I have a chance to begin, my iPhone rings. For a minute I think it might be Blake, except that I suspect it's quite early in the morning there. Then I hope it's Paige, although I don't know what I'd say. To my surprise though, it's Gabin.

"Oh, Gabin!" I exclaim in relief. "It's so good to hear your voice."

"Mon cheri!" he says happily. "And your voice is good too."

"I'm having a bad afternoon," I admit. "I'm in my room pouting."

"Pouting? That is not good. And it's beautiful weather. You

should be out enjoying Milan. Although you are correct, it is not as beautiful as Paris."

I stand up and look out the window. It really is gorgeous outside, all blue sky and sunshine, in a way that's probably unique to September. "It is lovely out there," I admit. "But I'm sorry to say my mood is cloudy and dark. I wouldn't be good company."

"I love your company," he tells me. "Come out and play, *cheri*. I will take you to my favorite *ristorante*."

"I'm not very hungry."

"We will first go and see sights," he says enticingly. "I know you love seeing the sights. You can bring your camera. I think the light is just about perfect."

I stare outside, knowing he's right. The light *is* perfect. "Okay, you talked me into it, Gabin."

"Fantastique!"

"Let me change." I pause. "Do I need to dress up?"

"You may dress however you please, *cheri*. No one will complain."

I thank him and hang up. Then I look in the closet. Out of respect for Gabin, I know I can't be too casual. Finally, I decide on a corduroy skirt with tights and a pair of Prada boots that Paige insisted I needed. I top this with a sweater and don't forget to add some accessories, following Paige's rule. Put several on then look in the mirror and take a couple of things off. "It's called editing," she likes to tell people. "Less is more."

Then I switch to a large Fendi bag, one of this morning's purchases, putting my camera and things into it. I head down to the lobby, where Gabin is already waiting. He smiles when he sees me. "You look beautiful," he says as he kisses my hand. "Casual yet stylish."

"Thank you," I tell him. "I tried."

We go straight outside, but instead of getting into a car, we head out on foot and I immediately begin to see some great photo opportunities with the architecture and the early evening light. Gabin is patient as I shoot here and there. He even points out some shots I might've missed and, all in all, I'm having a great time. I temporarily forget about why I was so out of sorts.

It's not until the sun is down and we're at dinner that I remember about my sister and what seems to me her doomed love life.

"Oh, oh," Gabin says to me after a bottle of red wine is placed on our table. "Here come the clouds again."

"Sorry." I attempt a smile. "It's really been a lovely evening."

"But I know you are troubled." He pours himself a glass of wine then looks curiously at me. "Are you still, as the English say, a teetotaler?"

I chuckle then hold my forefinger about an inch from my thumb. "I'll try a little."

"See, I thought I was right. I thought you were growing up, *cheri*."

"Well, as someone pointed out, Jesus' first miracle was turning water into wine. But I do think moderation is vital."

"As do I." He nods and holds up his glass. "Here is to friendship, *cheri*. Remember when you told me you wanted to be friends?"

"Yes."

"I did not respond so well then."

I make a nervous smile. "I remember."

"Maybe I too have grown up a little."

"Here's to friends," I say and we clink glasses. I take a sip and am surprised that it's not as bad as I expected. Still, it's not really my thing.

"Now, tell me, my friend," he says, his eyes serious. "What is troubling you?"

"I'll warn you," I begin. "It has to do with my sister. And I've really been trying to stay out of it. In fact, I'd love to stay out of it."

"But it is impossible?"

I nod. "Impossible." Then I tell him the whole thing—from Taylor's confession to what I saw while getting water this afternoon.

"You have not told this to Paige?"

"No." I shake my head. "To be honest, I haven't had an opportunity."

"And you say Dylan saw you ... seeing him?"

"Yes."

Gabin presses his lips together, concentrating. "It is possible that Dylan has already told Paige."

"Really?" I'm surprised by this. "You think Dylan would confess?"

"Perhaps not so much confess ... perhaps he has made a—how do you say? He has made defense ... explanation."

"Like putting his own spin on it?" I ask. "To make him seem innocent?"

"Yes. Like that. Perhaps he is excusing his, ah, his bad behavior. Do you think it is possible?"

"I think you could be right."

"And perhaps you must be careful what you say to Paige."

I take another sip of wine, mulling his advice in my brain. He may be French and he may have a different code of ethics than I do, but I do believe he's right about this. As I thank him for his advice and later, once again, for his friendship, I wonder if I was too quick to push this guy away last spring.

Chapter
17

Saturday is a busy day with back-to-back shows. As a result I never really get a private moment with Paige. And by the end of the day, I think maybe it's for the best. She seems so happy and oblivious that I think Dylan has either completely covered up what I saw yesterday or else has mentioned it in a dismissive way, like it was nothing. So if I mention it, she'll probably laugh and say I'm overreacting because I'm so moralistic and old-fashioned. Whatever the case, I decide to just bide my time.

"You and Gabin have to come to the after-party with Dylan and me tonight," Paige tells me as we're heading to our suite.

I already told her about spending time with Gabin last night. It was my only way to excuse having missed Dylan's after-party last night, although I'm sure he was relieved at my absence.

"It's a big party," she tells me. "Everyone will be there."

I can't even recall which Italian designer is hosting this particular event, but I know I don't want to be there. "I'm tired," I tell her. "I think I'd just like to spend the evening in."

"No way," she insists. "You played the hermit last night."

"I was out on the town with Gabin last night," I remind her. "Hardly a hermit. In fact, we had a wonderful time."

"You know what I mean, Erin." Paige is getting that stubborn look now, like she's about to pull a princess fit. "We are here for our show. Part of that includes making appearances. I need my sister by my side."

"You have Dylan by your side," I say in a flat voice.

She narrows her eyes slightly. "And that's a problem?"

I shrug then turn away.

"Mom said you were kind of down on him yesterday, Erin."

I feel slightly betrayed by this. What did Mom tell her? And why? Still, I'm not sure I want to go there right now.

"Mom said you thought his show wasn't very good."

I turn to face Paige, studying her closely. "What did *you* think of his show?"

She looks trapped—like no matter what she says, it will be wrong.

"Come on," I gently press her. "You're the fashion expert. If Dylan weren't your fiancée, what would you have said about his spring line? I'd like to know."

"Okay. I don't think those were his best designs."

I nod.

"I don't get why you'd hold that against him, Erin. That seems pretty mean and judgmental ... *even for you.*"

I blink. "Even for me?"

"Well, you know how you are. You've admitted it before. You can be pretty harsh and judgmental sometimes."

"So can you," I point out. "If a woman's purse is all wrong with her outfit, I've heard you—"

"I'm not talking about fashion now," she says loudly. "I'm talking about the way you judge someone's character."

"What if a person has *no* character?" I ask. "Am I supposed to simply pretend that he does have character?"

She looks stumped.

"Remember the old fairy tale 'The Emperor's New Clothes'?"

She shrugs, but I can tell by the look in her eyes she does remember it.

"Everyone was supposed to pretend the emperor looked fantastic," I say quickly, "but the foolish dork had been duped by a devious designer and he was actually parading around in his underwear. Remember?"

"And your point would be?"

"That's like Dylan."

"*What?*" she sputters.

"In fact, Dylan is like that in two ways."

"Explain yourself." Paige's voice is tight and high and I can tell she is about to explode. Even so, I continue.

"First of all there's Dylan's spring line, which is, in my opinion, ho-hum, unremarkable, and just plain boring. And yet you acted like it's inspired and amazing. I know you know better, Paige. You know it's not good, and yet you're acting like it is."

"It's because I believe in him," she insists. "He's an excellent designer. He got an early start and blew away some of his contemporaries. He was said to have the brightest future in the American industry and—"

"Maybe that was true then, but not so true now—"

"Who died and made you a fashion expert?" She glares at me.

"I'm just being honest, Paige. You're acting just like one of the emperor's subjects, pretending Dylan still has talent. And I know if it was anyone else's show, you would have cheerfully torn them to shreds."

"That's not—"

"Let me finish. Second of all there's Dylan himself—more specifically, his character, which in my opinion is seriously lacking. He plumps up his ego however he can. For all we know that could explain the decline of his creativity—"

"He's just having a little slump."

"And you're covering for him! That's my whole point, Paige, you're acting like one of the emperor's lame subjects. You're bowing down to Dylan and pretending like—"

"I am *not* bowing down to him!"

Suddenly I know I've gone too far. I'm not even sure how it happened. I've totally thrown Gabin's advice to the wayside. "I'm sorry," I say quietly.

"How can you say things like that, Erin?" She's right in my face and looks close to tears. "I'm your sister and you treat me like—"

"I'm saying it because I love you, Paige—"

"It's a strange way to show love, Erin!"

"It's because I don't want to see you get hurt."

"I'm not going to get hurt!"

"Yes." I nod firmly. "You are going to get hurt. Dylan is not who you think he is. He is definitely going to hurt you."

"You don't know what you're talking about."

"Even if I did ..." I pause, steadying myself, "would you listen?"

"You're just jealous," she says as she turns away, heading to the bathroom. "Just like all the other females in my life.

Everyone hates me because I'm successful and pretty and—"
She slams the door so loudly that I can't hear the last word.
And now water is running.

I sit down, wondering if I could've messed this up any
more, even if I'd tried. Once again, I pray. I pray that God will
somehow salvage my mess and help me communicate with
Paige in a way she can understand. Her shower finally ends
and I can hear the fan running, but she spends such a long
time in there that I feel worried.

By the time she emerges, looking fresh and perfect, I'm pacing. "Look," I say to her, "I'm really sorry for the way that went."

She smiles, but it's not genuine. "That's okay. I'm fine now."

"Good." I sit down and try to think.

"Should I assume that you and Gabin won't be going to
the after-party with Dylan and me tonight? I mean, I wouldn't
want to subject you to being seen with a second-rate designer
who has no character." Her voice cuts like acid.

"Oh, Paige." I stand and look at her. "Can I just explain
something to you? I mean calmly and without fireworks?"

"I don't know." She shrugs as she tightens the belt of her
bathrobe. "Can you?"

"I'd like to try."

"Fine." She sits on the sofa and I sit in the chair across
from her. "Go for it."

I begin by telling her what Taylor told me outside the
bathroom at the Nina Ricci after-party.

Paige looks stunned. "Seriously? Taylor said that?"

I nod. "She didn't say it proudly, and I can tell she still
cares about Dylan. She said he helped launch her career."

"That's true enough." She frowns. "I thought Taylor was
pretty ungrateful for leaving him in the lurch like that."

"Taylor is a Christian," I tell her. "And she didn't approve of Dylan acting like that toward her when he was engaged to you."

Paige folds her arms. "Well, to be fair, a lot of flirting goes on in the fashion world, Erin. People have to expect it."

"It sounded like more than flirting," I reply. "Dylan was coming on strong enough that Taylor was uncomfortable working for him."

"And a big opportunity just happened to come her way about the same time," Paige says dismissively. "Pretty handy if you ask me."

"I don't get that."

"Taylor wouldn't want to look selfish—dumping a designer who'd been good to her for one with a bigger name."

"But you know this industry," I point out. "Everyone is moving up, if they can."

"Maybe." She still looks unconvinced.

"I wasn't even going to tell you about that," I confess. "In fact, Gabin didn't think I should say—"

"Gabin knows about this?"

"Gabin's my friend," I say calmly. "He's been a good listener. A good adviser. And he admitted that he knew Dylan was like that."

"Like what?"

"Gabin said that Dylan spoke openly in France, admitting he loved beautiful women and—"

"Well, of course he loves beautiful women, Erin. He's a designer. Certainly you didn't think he'd love ugly women?" Her face registers more than a little impatience.

"That's not what Gabin meant."

"I would think you and Gabin could find more interesting things to talk about than Dylan and me."

"You're getting mad again," I point out. "I thought we were going to discuss this calmly."

"Whatever." She stands, going into the kitchen and getting a bottle of water.

"I have one more thing to tell you," I say slowly. "But I'm not going to tell you if you're already upset."

"Of course I'm upset, Erin. You're making some serious accusations about the man I love. Why wouldn't I be upset?"

"Okay." I stand, heading to the bathroom. "Let's just leave it at that then, because I'm sure you won't hear the rest of it anyway." And before she can respond I go into the bathroom, close the door, lean against it, and pray for help.

I stay in there about ten minutes and it's so quiet in the suite that I think Paige might've gotten dressed and left. But when I go back out, she's still in her bathrobe, sitting on the sofa again, sipping her water. "So ...?"

"You want to hear the rest?" I ask cautiously.

"Might as well get it over with," she says easily. "Then we can just forget about it and move on."

"Okay." I sit down again, taking in a deep breath. I tell her exactly what happened after Dylan's show yesterday, in detail, almost as if I'm in a court of law. When I finish, she doesn't say anything. She just sits there with a blank expression. I honestly don't have a clue how she feels. "Anyway ..." I hold up my hands. "I just thought you should know. I would want to know. I mean, if it were me."

"For your information, Dylan already told me about it."

"Oh." I nod stiffly. "Well, that's what Gabin said he would do."

"You told Gabin about this too? What else does Gabin know?"

"Sorry. I just needed to talk to someone."

"Anyway, for your information, Dylan explained the whole thing. He said that Cybil—that's the model he was comforting—was extremely upset because she had just found out her sister had died."

I stare at her in disbelief. "Really?"

She nods with a somber expression. "She was completely shattered by the news. And Dylan was simply comforting her. He said he saw you when you saw them and that he tried to say something to you, but that it looked like you'd assumed the very worst and ran off before he could explain what was going on."

"He said that, did he?" I'm trying to keep the skepticism out of my voice.

"He even said he could understand your reaction, Erin."

"Really?" I can't believe she's buying this.

"Yes." She makes a satisfied smile. "He was very gracious in defending you. He said that after all that Eliza nonsense, it was understandable that you would jump to a wrong conclusion. He knows you're protective of me. And he doesn't hold it against you. In fact, he suggested I discuss it with you."

"So this woman, did you meet her? Was Cybil at the after-party last night?"

"Of course not. She flew home to be with her family." Her brows arch as if to say, I told you so. "I would think you—*a Christian*—wouldn't be so quick to judge and condemn a person so unfairly."

"I see . . ." Now I'm second-guessing myself. Is it possible I perceived the situation wrong?

"I know you probably don't believe what I just told you," she says in a weary tone. "But, hopefully, you'll come to your senses."

I nod. "Yes ... hopefully."

"I suppose I can't talk you into going to the Baggatio after-party with us now?"

"I don't think so." I let out a long sigh. "I really am tired."

Paige looks at the clock. "Well, Dylan is taking me to dinner first. If you change your mind, just give me a call. We can always meet up later." She smiles in a sad way. "And, really, no hard feelings. Dylan is right—it's understandable that you would feel defensive of me, Erin. I mean, seriously, if you caught Dylan doing something—well, like you thought—I would want you to tell me. I would want you to come running."

"Really?" I'm surprised by this. "You wouldn't just think that ignorance is bliss?"

Paige looks like I've lost my mind. "Are you kidding? What girl wants to be involved with a cheater?"

"Not me," I tell her.

"And most definitely not me." She shakes her head. "Now I need to get dressed."

I experience a mixture of feelings after Paige leaves. On the one hand, I'm glad we ended on a relatively peaceful note. On the other hand, I'm confused. Is it possible that I read this whole thing wrong? And what about what Taylor said? And Gabin? Finally, I decide there's nothing else I can do—well, except to pray for Paige and Dylan. After that, I need to just let it be.

Chapter
18

It's a little past seven when my phone rings. Once again it's Gabin, and when I tell him I'm not interested in going out tonight, he is disappointed.

"Are you going to stay in and be sad?"

"Who says I'm sad?" I ask.

"I can hear it in your voice, *cheri*."

"Oh." I tell him about my conversation with Paige and how it turned out Gabin was right. "Or maybe I was wrong," I admit. "Dylan actually seemed to have a pretty good explanation for what I saw."

"And you believe him?"

"I'm not sure. But I'm not sure I have a choice."

"Perhaps not."

"At least Paige and I are okay," I tell him.

"And yet you are sad."

"Maybe so." I realize my sadness is twofold now. Part of it's related to Paige and Dylan. And part of it is Blake's silence—and this strong sense that we are really over.

"Come out with me," he urges. "I will help you forget sad."

I have to chuckle at his English. "I'm not sure you could do that, Gabin."

"Come on, *cheri*," he pleads. "This is Milan. Perhaps not as beautiful as Paris. But no place for sadness."

"Okay," I agree.

"Splendid! I know just the place. Put on a pretty dress, *cheri*. We will dance tonight."

I'm not sure how I feel about dancing, but it might be a good way to forget about Paige and Dylan. So I hunt through the closet and the freestanding clothes rack until I find what looks like a decent dancing dress. It's a Nina Ricci lacey number in a soft periwinkle blue. Very feminine, with a skirt that can swirl. I find a pair of bronze-colored platform shoes and, although I'm not sure what Paige would say, I think they look okay. I may not be ready for the cover of *Couture*, but I'll bet I'm more stylish than anyone in Dylan's last show. Not that I want to obsess over that.

In the elevator is a dark-haired woman in a hot-pink cocktail dress. She's very beautiful and obviously a model, but something about her is strikingly familiar too. And then, somewhere between the third and second floor, it hits me. I know who she is.

"Is your name Cybil?" I ask pleasantly.

"Yes." She nods and smiles happily. Perhaps a bit too happily. "That is me — Cybil." Her accent is thick, and I'm guessing she's from an eastern bloc country.

"I'm Erin," I say, trying to think of a way to continue the conversation. "I cohost an American TV show about fashion."

Her eyes light up. "Oh! That is nice!"

"Yes. Did I see you in the Marceau show yesterday?"

"Yes!" She nods eagerly. "That is right."

"You're very good," I tell her as the elevator doors open. "Very talented."

"Thank you!"

We step outside the elevator and I place my hand on her arm. "I was sorry to hear about your sister."

Her dark eyes cloud with confusion. "My *sister*?"

"Oh. Maybe I'm thinking of someone else."

"I have *no* sister. Just three brothers." She laughs and holds her hand above her. "Such big boys, they are. All more tall than me."

I laugh to imagine brothers taller than her—she must be close to six feet. "I'll bet they're protective of you."

"Protective?" She considers this word then nods eagerly. "Yes!"

Suddenly I get an idea. "Hey, are you going to an after-party tonight?"

"Yes!" She smiles, revealing perfect white teeth. "Baggatio, *no*?"

"Yes." I smile back. "That's the one I'm going to."

"I *am* going." She nods eagerly.

"Great," I tell her. "I will look for you there."

"Super!"

She walks across the lobby, joining a small group of other models, and I wave to Gabin. Hurrying over to him, I breathlessly explain my brief elevator conversation. Then I tell him about my sudden change of plans. "I'm sorry, but I have to go to that after-party now."

"I understand. It is like *fate*."

"Or God," I say.

He nods soberly. "I believe God controls fate."

"Hopefully God will help me do what I have to do." I make a stiff smile. "Because I know it won't be easy."

"So . . . no dancing tonight?"

"I have to do this, Gabin."

"Perhaps you need an escort?"

"Really? You'd do that for me?"

He smiles. "If it makes you happy."

"We don't have to stay long," I promise him as we head out to grab a taxi. "But I *have* to do this, Gabin. Paige told me if I ever caught Dylan cheating on her that I was supposed to run to her and tell her."

"Then we will run." He waves to a taxi down the street, and we literally run and hop into it. After about fifteen minutes, we pull into a circular driveway in front of a beautiful stone mansion. I'm not even sure my name's on the guest list, but I'm hoping, between Gabin and me, that one of us can gain access. Otherwise, I'll use Paige's name. But Gabin steps up and, after a few words with the gatekeeper, has no problem getting us into the party.

"I don't want to go directly to Paige," I say as we make our way through the oversized foyer.

"You have a plan?" he asks with interest.

"First I want to make sure Paige is here. Then I'll need to find Cybil again," I say. "After that I want to introduce Cybil to Paige."

He makes a nervous smile. "I am at your disposal."

I lead him around from room to room, checking out the guests and looking for my sister. Finally, I am fairly sure that Paige and Dylan must still be lingering over dinner. So I point to where a jazz ensemble is playing by the entrance to an enchanting courtyard that's magically lit with strings of fairy lights garlanded around the trees. A few couples are already dancing.

"You said you wanted to dance tonight," I remind Gabin. He takes my hand and leads me out. As we dance, I try to keep an eye on people moving in and around the rooms. It's not long before I see Cybil and her pretty friends milling about, but I still haven't spotted Paige and Dylan. I just hope they haven't changed their minds.

After a few dances, we take a break and sample the food, which is mouthwatering, as usual. "I'm worried," I tell Gabin. "It's possible that Dylan and Paige aren't coming."

"It is possible." He tips his head toward the foyer. "Except that is them, coming in now."

"Really?" I feel my heartbeat quicken.

"Yes. They have stopped to talk with the host."

"I need to find Cybil," I say quickly. "Will you wait here and keep an eye on them from a distance? Please, don't let them leave if you can help it."

He nods. "I am your partner in espionage."

I make my way through the room, which is growing increasingly crowded, searching through the hordes of beautiful tall women for Cybil and her friends. I know Cybil has on a hot-pink dress, which should be easy to spot. After a few minutes I locate her. Taking a calming breath, I casually approach the chattering group of women. They are speaking in another language, but to my relief, Cybil notices me and smiles.

"Oh, here you are," she says cheerfully. "This is the woman," she tells her friends. "The one with *American television show*." She introduces me to her friends, who greet me in equally thick accents. I visit briefly with them then turn my attention back to Cybil.

"Were you at the Dylan Marceau after-party last night?" I ask her.

She shakes her head no, then giggles. "I was at *after* after-party," she tells me in a confidential tone, and I think I get her meaning.

"In that case, there is someone you *must* meet tonight," I declare.

Her eyes widen hopefully. "Yes?"

"Do you have a few minutes?"

She smiles. *"Oh, yes!"*

I have mixed feelings as I lead Cybil through the throng, searching for Paige and desperately hoping I can pull this off without making a horrible mess. It's not that I want anyone to get hurt ... not any more than they've hurt themselves already. But I do want to enlighten my sister. Finally, I spot Paige talking to one of the Baggatio under-designers. To my relief, Dylan isn't with her.

"There she is," I tell Cybil, without pointing directly to Paige, just in case Cybil knows who she is. "An American fashion expert." I move in quickly now, stepping right next to Paige. "Excuse me." I tap her on the shoulder, interrupting her conversation in mid-sentence.

She turns to me with surprised eyes but then smiles. "I'm so glad you came tonight, Erin."

"There's someone you *must* meet," I say with manufactured enthusiasm.

Her eyes brighten. *"Who?"*

I nod to Cybil. *"This* is Cybil," I say calmly.

Paige's brows arch. *"Cybil?"*

Cybil seems oblivious. "Yes. I am Cybil."

"This is my sister," I tell Cybil.

Cybil takes Paige's hand. "I am most pleased to meet you."

Paige looks confused.

"Cybil is a very talented model," I say quickly, glancing at Cybil, who is still smiling. "But Cybil's not as lucky as I am. Cybil does not *have* a sister." I turn to Cybil, who seems a bit confused. "Right?"

"Right . . ." She nods. "I have no sister."

"But you have three brothers?"

"Yes!" She smiles. "Three brothers."

"Cybil." Paige speaks slowly. "Did you model for Dylan Marceau?"

Cybil's pretty smile gets even bigger. "Oh, yes. Yes, I did."

Dylan steps up with two glasses of champagne, handing one to Paige with a smile. I'm sure he hasn't noticed Cybil yet and I'm not sure of my next move, but I'm determined not to let him slither out of this. "Dylan," I say pleasantly, "I was just introducing Paige to Cybil."

Dylan's jaw stiffens as he barely tips his head toward me in a silent greeting. His eyes dart toward Cybil, then away.

"Cybil was just telling us how she has *no sisters*." I shake my head sadly. "It's a shame too, because Cybil's sisters would probably be as beautiful as Cybil." I smile at her.

"You are too kind," she says to me.

"You have no idea," I tell her.

"But you are right," she continues. "I have no sister. Just me and my three big brothers." She smiles at Dylan, her eyes twinkling as if she's extremely glad to see him tonight.

I tap Cybil on the arm, redirecting her attention back to Paige. "Now that you've met my sister, did you know that she is engaged to marry Dylan Marceau?"

With a creased brow, Cybil looks from Dylan to Paige. She's clearly confused—probably as blindsided as Paige, which makes me sad. "No ... I did not," she says. All the sparkle is gone from her eyes.

"I didn't think you did," I tell her.

Suddenly Cybil looks at Paige with frightened eyes. It's obvious that she knows that Paige knows. "I am—I am *sorry*."

"No ..." Paige says slowly. "I'm the one who's sorry." She puts a hand on Cybil's arm, looking up into her eyes. *"Do you want Dylan?"*

Cybil looks like she's about to pass out or make a run for it, but she just stands there.

"Because you can have him."

"I—uh—I—" Cybil's hand flies to her mouth.

Paige turns to Dylan. "You lied to me, didn't you?"

Not surprisingly, he is speechless.

Paige lifts her glass of champagne as if to make a toast, but instead she tosses the contents onto Dylan. Then she hands me the empty glass, twists the big diamond off her finger, and shoves it into Dylan's hand. *"We are finished!"* Paige glances around to see that everyone within about a twenty-foot radius is staring at us. She turns back to Dylan. "And my sister and I are of the opinion that your design career is finished too." She stands tall. *"Ciao!"*

Paige nudges me to turn around then links her arm through mine, probably to steady herself as we walk away. I'm shocked to spot Eliza in the crowd of onlookers—her jaw is literally dropped. I toss her a look—like *see what kind of person Dylan really is.* Or maybe she knows. I don't really care. I just want out of here.

To my relief, Gabin hurries straight to us, moving to Paige's other side. He takes her free arm, and together we escort her toward the foyer. I can feel how wobbly her steps are and by the time we're outside the front door, where we find a bench in a shadowy spot alongside the driveway, Paige collapses.

While Gabin calls for a taxi, I hold my sister, letting her cry on my shoulder as I tell her, "It'll be okay ... it'll be okay." And I believe it will be okay—in time, anyway. But as I hear my sister sobbing, I'm not so sure about the short term.

Chapter
19

Paige does a commendable job of making it through the next three days in Milan. Really, the girl deserves an Emmy. Even when handling the paparazzi, who are all over this story, she is classy and gracious and even slightly humorous. As a result the press is eating her up—in a good way.

Even our mom seems to buy her act. But in the privacy of our suite, Paige becomes another person. I've heard the expression "a shadow of oneself," and that's how she seems to me. Paige's shadow quietly brushes her teeth, gets a bottle of water, and goes to bed ... all while barely saying three words. At first I tried to cheer her up, but now I just give her space. I don't even mind that we've skipped the last two after-parties.

Of course, Mollie, who as usual is tuned into Facebook and the latest celeb gossip, texted me for details regarding the breakup. I texted her back, saying that, although Paige was blue, she was fortunate to have found out the truth and escaped Dylan before it was too late. Then Mollie texted me back saying that she was praying for Paige, and she even asked me to give my sister a great big hug from her and Fern. I had to smile at that—it sounds like Mollie is returning to her old self and that's encouraging.

And Mollie's not the only one who's doing better these days. I spoke with Fran on the phone yesterday and it sounds as if she gets stronger each day. She told me she's certain that she'll be able to come with us on our next trip. "As long as your mom still wants to co-direct," she told me. I assured her that Mom was fully onboard with the show now—and that I thought they would make a good team.

I was a little surprised to get a TM from Blake too. Especially since he's been so silent since I got to Milan. But in usual Blake style (at least since his involvement in the new reality show), his text was brief and to the point. He said that Paige was lucky to be rid of Dylan (of course, I totally agree with that) and then he basically said that all twenty-somethings should just take a break from serious relationships—period. At first I couldn't figure that part of the message out. Was this his subtle way of telling me that he doesn't want to be involved with me again? But that's crazy since we're not involved anyway. Or maybe things with Grace have been disappointing for him. The fact is, I haven't really given Blake that much thought the last few days. It's like I really do think that whatever I had with him, or thought I had with him, truly is over. Finito.

This is probably one of the main reasons I've really enjoyed spending time with Gabin. And, thanks to Paige's disinterest in attending the after-parties, Gabin and I have been spending the past few evenings together. He's shown me more of Milan than I thought possible in these past three days. And last night, our last evening together, when we parted ways in the lobby, he asked if it was okay for us to stay in touch.

"I would love that," I told him.

"And perhaps I will see you during New York Fall Fashion Week?"

"I hope so."

Then he asked what I would think if he came to visit me in LA sometime. "Perhaps if the company is doing something there."

"That would be cool," I told him. "Then I could be *your* tour guide."

"I would be visiting you as your friend," he assured me.

I smiled. "I'd like that."

"I know." He touched my cheek. "And it is possible that friends someday become more than friends?"

"I think it's very possible," I assured him. "But I do believe friendship is the best way to start any relationship."

His eyes lit up. "You have made me very happy, Erin."

Just then I felt my heart give a little surge ... a surge that made me wonder. Perhaps Gabin and I will become something more ... when the timing is right. Then he kissed my hand and we both said "Ciao" and parted ways.

This morning, I feel sad that I won't see Gabin again for a while. I'm also a bit relieved. I need some time and space to think about this—to decide how I really feel about a long-distance relationship and all that could mean. Because the truth is I'm just not sure.

What I am sure of is that I'm happy that we're packing to go home. Most of our things will be shipped, but we still have to round up our personal items and get them ready to travel.

"I'm not sure I can handle the paparazzi today," Paige tells me after the bellhop picks up our larger luggage. Mom and Leah are already downstairs, checking us out of our rooms and overseeing the loading of the car.

"Maybe I can deal with them for you," I suggest. "Or you could go incognito. Although I'd think with so many tall, gorgeous women checking out, you should be able to blend in."

But she decides to go with a disguise and, because most of our bags are gone, we decide to do some quick swapping. I switch my tweed menswear blazer, which is so not like her, for her gorgeous Chanel jacket. I also let her wear my fedora-style hat, which she tucks her hair into. Then she dons her oversized Gucci shades. And despite all that, she still looks stylish.

"Even in that getup you look totally fashionable," I tell her. How does she do it?

"Why don't you go down ahead of me?" she suggests. "That might help some."

So I head down first, finding Mom and Leah waiting in the foyer. I explain that Paige is trying to slip beneath the paparazzi radar. But we wait and wait and she still doesn't show up.

"Are you sure she's okay?" Mom asks with frightened eyes. "I know how depressed she is."

I feel concerned too. Not that I think Paige would really do anything stupid, but I do know she's not herself. "I'll go check," I tell Mom and hurry toward the elevators. Just as I reach the suite, Paige opens the door and I can tell that she's been crying.

"Are you okay?" I ask with concern.

She just nods.

"What happened?"

"Dylan called."

"Oh." My mind immediately starts running in circles. This is the first she's heard from him since the night she said they were finished.

"He apologized."

"Oh." I can't think of anything else to say. But I'm worried.

"He begged me to forgive him."

I go inside the suite, closing the door. I know Paige wants to talk, but I'm wordless.

"He said that he's really sorry," she continues.

I nod, waiting.

"And he wants me to take him back."

"Oh," I say for the third time.

"He admitted that he has a problem, Erin."

"Right ... that's good."

"He said I'm the only woman he's ever truly loved—that the rest were just flings, that he doesn't want to live his life like that."

"And what did you say?"

"I was kind of dumbfounded. I mean, I've been so angry at him ... so hurt and humiliated. I didn't ever want to see him or hear his voice again. I was done."

"That's understandable."

"But he made me feel guilty."

"He made *you* feel guilty?"

"Kind of."

"For what?" I'm trying to keep my temper controlled, but it's not easy.

Paige sits on the sofa. "Well ... I decided to take your advice, Erin."

I blink. "*My* advice? About what?"

"You know ... what you said about premarital sex. I got to thinking that maybe God really did have a good reason for wanting us to wait. And, like you said, maybe it was the best way to avoid unnecessary heartache."

"Really?"

"I told Dylan that. As soon as I saw him here in Milan I made it clear that I didn't want to have sex with him during this trip."

I nod, trying not to show my surprise.

"Naturally, he wasn't pleased."

"Naturally."

"And today he told me that Cybil had been coming on to him the whole time—and because I was, well, *withholding* is what he called it, that was why he hooked up with Cybil."

"And you believe that?"

Paige shakes her head. "No. I'm not a fool, Erin."

I let out a relieved sigh. "I didn't think you were."

"I told him that his choice to cheat was just that—his choice. It had nothing to do with me. Well, except that it hurt me. I told him that he had a fidelity problem that he needed to own up to. I even suggested that he might have a sexual addiction." She makes a half smile. "That might've been an overstatement on my part."

I shrug. "Or not. It seems clear that he's had some problems, Paige."

"Yes. That's what I told him. And that I meant what I said on Saturday night—we are done. Finished. I will never go back with him. I will never marry him. End of story."

I control myself from jumping up and down and cheering. "Good for you, Paige. You deserve someone who will treat you better than that. Lots better."

"I know. Even so, this hurts. And I felt so bad when Dylan started crying. It's hard hearing a guy sob. I know he's in almost as much pain as I am. Maybe even more."

"That might be good for him," I say hopefully. "If he's really hurting, he might rethink his life and some of his bad choices. He might make some genuine changes."

"Yes. But even if he does change, I will never go back to him. I really am done. There's nothing he can say or do to win me back."

I sit on the sofa and hug her. "I'm so relieved for your sake, Paige. I know it must hurt, but I'm really glad for you. And I know that in time, you'll feel better."

She sniffs. "I feel better now."

I look at my watch. "We should go."

She walks to where her carry-on and bag are sitting by the terrace door, but then she just stands there looking out. "You know, it feels like I barely saw Milan … like I wasn't really here." She shakes her head. "And it's really beautiful, isn't it?"

"It is." I reach for her carry-on. "I guess that's how life is sometimes."

"How?"

"We miss out on the beauty when we're distracted with the messy parts."

"Like messy relationships?"

"Yeah."

"But you had a good time in Milan, didn't you?" she asks. "You went out and saw the sights and things?"

"I did. It's an amazing city. This history, the architecture, the food, it's all really cool."

She turns and looks at me. "I know you're the younger sister, Erin, but I think it's about time I started to learn some things from you."

I shrug. "I know I've learned a lot of things from you."

She smiles. "You mean from my mistakes?"

"Sometimes. But I've learned a lot of other good things

too. And I'm not just talking about style either, although you've taught me some about that. But there's more to you than just fashion."

"I hope so." She sighs. "And I hope I can start getting in touch with some of it too."

"Maybe we can help each other," I tell her.

"Absolutely."

"Ciao, Milan!" I say to the scene outside the window, turning away.

"Ciao," she echoes, picking up her bag.

"Here's to happier days," I say as we leave the suite.

"And to sisterhood," she says as we walk to the elevator.

While the elevator goes down to the lobby, I silently ask God to make me into the kind of sister Paige needs—to love her unconditionally and to share my life and my beliefs with her. Because, more than ever I realize that—at least for now—guys will come and go in our lives ... but sisters truly are forever.

DISCUSSION QUESTIONS
FOR *CIAO*

1. The title of this last book in the series is *Ciao*. What do you think the girls are saying good-bye to? Are they also saying hello to anything?
2. When Fran's mother moves in to take care of her daughter, Erin is stuck playing mediator. She has to respect Mrs. Bishop's feelings while still keeping Fran's best interest in mind. Do you think she succeeds? How would you have balanced this type of relationship?
3. Paige says she and Erin "rub off on each other." Erin says, "I try to get Paige to think more realistically and she tries to get me to loosen up." How well do you think this type of relationship works? What traits of Erin do you see rubbing off on Paige? Does more than Paige's fashion sense rub off on Erin?
4. Paige confronts Eliza about her time with Dylan in the Bahamas. Do you think Paige handled the situation well? Do you think she deserved to get revenge on Eliza?
5. While on Blake and Ben's reality dating show, Erin is overdressed for her blind date. If you were in her situation and felt uncomfortable, how would you react?
6. When doing a shopping segment for their show, Erin states, "I can't help think of how unrealistic these portions of our 'reality' show really are … Yet here we are, shopping at Gucci like we're made of money." Based on this comment, what do you think the show *On the Runway* represents?
7. In what way have the Forrester sisters changed since *Premiere*? Who has changed more—Erin or Paige? Explain.
8. While in Milan, the girls' mother wonders if Erin has commitment issues. Erin admits to having wondered about this before as well. Does this change your perception of Erin? In what ways could this possibly explain

Erin's actions (not wanting to commit to Blake in the beginning of the series, only wanting to be friends with Gabin, etc.)?

9. Erin's always been leery her friends' relationships. For instance, she wonders if both Benjamin and Dylan were right for Paige, and she is unsure if Mollie should get back together with Tony. Do you think Erin has a right to be suspicious of the guys' intentions, or is her advice to her friends regarding their relationships only a projection of her own fear of getting hurt?

10. Mollie thinks Erin and Paige have the perfect lives. If you were Erin, is there anything you could do for Mollie to make her feel more included?

11. At the end of the series Erin recognizes designers and is able to throw together a stylish outfit without her sister's help. Does this change speak to her growth as a fashionista? Is it a positive change in Erin? Why or why not?

12. How do you think the series would have been different if told from Paige's point of view?

ON THE RUNWAY

A Novel

PREMIERE

Bestselling Author
Melody
Carlson

Chapter 1

"Here we are at wonderful Wonderland." Paige doesn't even blink as she flashes a bright smile at the camera crew before launching into a clever monologue about the local theme park and its recent improvements. I'm sure I'm one of the few present who knows her real opinion on this mediocre park. "This is so last century," she told our mom earlier today. But now she is all sunshine as she espouses the park's many "wonders."

Meanwhile, a small crowd gathers around her, looking on with interest like she's a celebrity. They're chatting amongst themselves and nodding toward her like they're trying to figure out just who she is. But the problem is she's *not anybody*. Well, she's my sister. And, in her own eyes, she's a soon-to-be-discovered star. But then who isn't down here in La La Land, CA, where it seems half the girls I know have a bad case of celebrity-itis? They either want to be famous themselves or connected to someone who already is famous.

I would never admit this to Paige, but she's got the look of a star. Not to mention the attitude. Plus, she knows how to dress. And it doesn't hurt that she's got peaches and cream skin, straight white teeth, clear blue eyes, and nearly natural blonde hair that despite being long always looks perfect. Not unlike her old Barbie doll. Some people have compared Paige's looks to Cameron Diaz, but in all fairness, Paige might even be prettier. Not that you'll hear those words coming from my mouth anytime soon. And certainly not while Paige is within hearing distance. I love my sister, but that girl's head is big enough already.

Anyway, as usual, I am hiding behind my video camera, acting as if I'm a member the Channel Five camera crew, although I'm fully aware that this is live coverage and my shots will not be used. Still, it's good practice as well as my best excuse to remain behind the scenes—or in other words, *in my comfort zone.* Not only that, but my camera helps to cover the conspicuous pimple that's threatening to erupt on my forehead today. Okay, so I am a little self-conscious and a bit insecure when it comes to my looks. But who wouldn't be with someone like Paige for a sister?

As I zoom in on Paige's picture-perfect face, I notice that the wind has blown a silky strand of hair across her highly glossed lips, and it sticks there like a fly on flypaper. She casually peels the strand off and continues to rattle on about the park's new and improved amenities, like it's no big deal.

"It's the twenty-fifth anniversary here at Wonderland." She addresses the camera. "And crowds have gathered here today to celebrate the reopening of the recently renovated theme park. More than two million dollars were spent bringing the park back to its former glory and, as you can see, everything looks clean and new and idyllic."

I try not to be overly wowed with my sister's natural gift for gab, but sometimes the girl totally floors me. How does she do it? Still, I never let on that I'm impressed. By the same token, I never let on that I'm intimidated. Not even by her looks. It's not that I'm a dog. My friends all assure me that I'm relatively attractive. But, hey, they're my friends. What else are they going to say?

The cameras continue to roll and Paige rambles on, and she's starting to get this look in her eye, almost like she's become bored with her subject matter. Not that I blame her. I mean, there's only so much you can say about a second-rate theme park, no matter how much money they throw at it.

Fortunately for Paige, my mom is signaling for her to wrap it up by slashing her hand across her throat and mouthing "cut." And Paige, used to this routine, makes her graceful exit. "And now back to the anchor desk at Channel Five News."

"That was good," Mom tells her, but her eyes are on the monitor and I can tell by her expression that she's listening to her headset, probably taking direction from someone back at the station. She nods and says, "Okay. Sure, no problem, we can do that." Then she turns back to the camera crew. "They want us to get a few more minutes of airtime—they decided to cut the trucker story. So we'll be back on in fifteen. Everybody hang tight."

"What more can I say about Wonderland?" Paige demands, letting out a sigh that sounds like she just ran a five-minute mile. Sometimes my sister can be a real prima donna.

"I don't know," Mom says absently. She's still listening to her headset as if there's another big story she should be going after. "Just ad lib, okay?"

"How about if we go shoot near the entrance," suggests Sam Holliday. Sam's the head cameraman and a very nice guy, as well as the first person to let me handle a real camera.

Mom nods. "Good idea. Maybe we can get some of the park's guests to say a few words and give Paige a break." Now Mom points to me. "Or perhaps Erin can take a turn being on camera."

This is all it takes to make my sister stand up and take notice. And I know her well enough to see that she is not ready to share the limelight with anyone—especially me. And this, I must admit, is a relief.

"I'll interview some guests." Paige takes the second mic and we head over to the entrance area. We're barely set up when Mom gives Paige the signal to start. Then Mom heads off to use her cell phone.

"Here we are again for the big reopening of Wonderland," Paige says with another brilliant smile. "As you can see the people are *pouring* into the theme park this afternoon." An overstatement since there are about six people trickling in at the moment. "And here's a fresh idea—since the Golden Globes are next month, let's pretend like this is the red carpet and we are on *fashion watch*."

Then with mic in hand, Paige approaches a couple of unsuspecting teenage girls. They look a bit wary as to whether they want to be on TV or not, but my sister quickly disarms them by smiling and saying, "Welcome to Wonderland, girls. Is this your first time here?"

One girl nods without speaking, but the other girl is a little braver. "Yeah. We decided to come since it was half price today."

"And did you get those Capri pants for half price as well?" asks Paige. Well, I almost drop my camera, except that I'm curious to record the girl's reaction and I have to admit the baggy, white cropped pants were a bad choice. Not only do they make her butt look big, but there's a spill stain on one knee.

The girl looks shocked, but her friend just nudges her with an elbow, then giggles. "Yeah," the friend tells Paige, "she *did* get them on sale. How'd you know that?"

Paige smiles slyly. "Oh, it's a gift. So how would you describe your fashion style today?" she asks the half-price girl who seems to be speechless. "Campy casual or theme park comfort or thrift shop chic?"

"Uh, I guess it's theme park comfort," the girl mutters.

"Well, comfort *is* important," says Paige, turning to the other girl. "And how about you?" she asks. The girl frowns down at her black T-shirt. It's well worn with a faded white skull on the front. "Sort of revisited Goth perhaps?"

I wince inwardly but keep my camera focused and running. In a twisted way this is actually kind of good.

The girl shrugs. "Yeah ... it's an old shirt."

"And it's just *adorable* on you," says Paige, "and it reminds me of the good old days." She's smiling back at the camera now and totally ignoring our mom, who is off the phone now, but freaking out as she sends all kinds of throat slashing "cut-cut-cut" signals Paige's direction, although no one is paying attention. I actually think the camera crew is enjoying Paige's little spectacle—or else they're too shocked to shut it down.

"And I'll be the first one to admit that fashion is subjective," Paige continues. "After all, this is only a theme park. But on the other hand, you just never know who you might bump into." She laughs then turns back to the camera. "As you can all see everyone is having a fabulous time at Wonderland today. They've put on their very best togs and are parading about for the world to enjoy."

Then Paige continues to describe outfits, turning what was supposed to be theme park coverage into a great big *What*

Not to Wear spot. And by the time the camera crew finally does shut down after five long minutes of Paige's merciless attacks, Mom's face is getting those weird red blotches—not a good sign.

"Paige Forrester!" Mom seethes. "What on earth do you think you were doing?"

"Ad libbing," Paige says lightly.

Sam chuckles as he pats Mom on the back. "Don't worry, Brynn," he tells her, "who really watches the five o'clock news anyway?"

Mom turns and actually glares at him now. "Well, have no doubts that this piece will be cut out of the six o—" But she cuts herself off to listen to her headset again. Now she's grimacing as if someone back at the station is speaking way too loudly. Make that yelling, because I can hear him fairly well and it sounds a lot like her boss, Max. And the words he's using would not be acceptable on the air.

"You probably got Mom fired," I whisper to Paige.

Her brows crease slightly. "No, you don't really think—"

"I didn't *put* her up to anything," Mom says loudly. "Listen, Max, I—" But she's interrupted again and we can all hear him shouting.

I fold my camera closed and shake my head at Paige. "See what you did?"

Paige nods without speaking and her eyes look worried. For some reason this makes me feel a tiny bit better about my sister's sensibility, or rather lack of it. Still, I'm wondering what we would really do if Mom lost her job. It's only been three years since Dad died and our world was turned upside down. Since that time, Mom has worked long and hard to gain respect at the station—enough respect to land her this producing job about six months ago. And despite her hard work, there are still some Channel Five employees who think she got her promotion out of pity … simply because her husband (our dad), Dan Forrester, the beloved anchor on the Channel Five news for more than a decade, had been tragically killed in a plane wreck. To think that Paige could've messed this all up in just a few minutes is seriously disturbing.

On the Runway Series
from Melody Carlson

When Paige and Erin Forrester are offered their own TV show, sisterly bonds are tested as the girls learn that it takes two to keep their once-in-a-lifetime project afloat.

Premiere
Book One

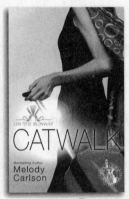

Catwalk
Book Two

Rendezvous
Book Three

Spotlight
Book Four

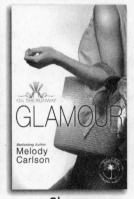

Glamour
Book Five

Ciao
Book Six

Available in stores and online!